KEYS TO HIS HEART

AUTHORESS LEM

Keys to His Heart

Published by Mz. Lady P Presents

QUOTE

The fight between your heart and mind is always the worst especially when walking away is the only option you have left...

CHECK THEM OUT

*Contact **MakeupbyDaria** for all your makeup needs.*
*Download music by **Jokaboi** and **Lawlucas***

ONE
BREEZE

"Be mindful of the person who carry that bone," my best friend Diamond said.

I had been on the phone with her for hours, going over the weekend drama. Diamond was the homebody type, but my friend was always one call away. I was the one who was always in the streets, but whenever I called, she was there, standing right behind me in the crossfire.

I picked up the phone and called her as soon as the sun came up. I was beyond pissed at the things that had been going on lately, but last night, all bets were off, and muthafuckas had really crossed the lines.

"I don't even understand why you still dealing with that bullshit. You are extremely too smart and beautiful to let a bunch of broke muthafuckas play with you." I heard everything Diamond was saying, and I knew she was telling the truth. However, my heart was stuck. No matter how many times I got up and walked away from it all, my heart said, "*Stay.*" I had been betrayed, used, talked about, and lied on, but I placed my loyalty above it all.

"I'ma get up with you later," I softly spoke.

"Breeze, don't shut me out again." I had a bad habit of shutting everyone out when I had an emotional breakdown which occurred very often. Instead of responding, I hung up. At this point, I was done with it all. I wasn't in a good head space, and I needed to get my thoughts together. I wasn't going to shut Diamond out, though, I just needed to be alone.

I powered my phone off and fell deep in my thoughts. Imagine going from the girl everyone liked to the girl everyone hated. My name is Breeze McGuy, and at the age of nineteen, I'd seen it all. It was crazy how life worked, and the hand God sometimes dealt you, but with my current events, I just looked at them as blessings. Something big was about to happen in my life, and God had eliminated the fake in order for me to prosper.

Lately, things had been bad. My love life was nonexistent, and the only friend I had by my side was Diamond. She made me mad just thinking about how dirty they had done me. It was like everyone started looking down on me like I was nothing. Moreover, the man I was deeply in love with just moved on, saying fuck me. What was I to do at this point? I was weak and hurting, but the crazy part was, nobody had seen how bad I was hurting.

Feeling that I was too deep in thought, I sat up in bed and immediately began to cry. I knew my mom had to be turning over in her grave right now. She had passed away when I was ten, and I then went to live with my grandmother. I didn't know my father, and since he had never reached out to me before, I didn't think to give him the time of day when he tried two years ago after my grandmother had passed. All this time with no father was great, so I didn't need one now. I took care of myself the best way I knew how. I got a job at Burger King and stayed in income-based apartments. Life wasn't the best, but not one time did I complain. I knew better days were ahead.

With everything going on, I grabbed my phone off the crate that sat by the bed and powered it back on. I looked at the number for at least ten minutes before dialing my father's number and accepting his offer to move to Atlanta with him. He had promised me new beginnings, and the way things were going, I needed one. A few minutes later, he sent me a plane ticket. Being that I didn't have much, it took me no time to pack up. I called an Uber, and just as easy as I had come in, I left out without saying so much as a goodbye. The way I saw it, everyone hated me so no one would notice I was gone.

On the way to the airport, I rolled down the window and threw my phone out the window. *Starting over from scratch shouldn't be bad,* I thought to myself, followed by a giggle, right before I drifted off to sleep.

TWO
BREEZE
SEVEN YEARS LATER

"You ready, Boss?" my right-hand man, Relle, asked me.

It had been so long since I had stepped foot in White Castle. The day I left, I ended all contact with everyone, only speaking to Diamond and a few of my family members. I didn't want to ever step foot back in this place, but Diamond was getting married, and I had promised her I wouldn't miss her wedding for anything in the world. Only death could have changed that, and I wasn't dying any time soon. A bitch like me was rare, so for that alone, it would take hell and high water to get me up out of here.

"Yeah, I got an appointment with makeupbyDaria for 3:00, and it's already 2:30."

Life for me had been great. It turned out making that call to my dad was one of the best decisions I had ever made. So many times, I wanted to ask him why he had never reached out to me, but at this point, the only thing that mattered was him being here right now.

It didn't take me long to figure out what my father did for a living after pulling up to his mini-mansion, which was heavily guarded. My father was just a street man. He stayed home, only leaving when he was needed. At that point, I knew he was higher up than a little drug dealer. He had some of the purest cocaine ever, and he had taught me the game. After being taught everything, it wasn't long before niggas feared me.

"You know you gotta meet up with them cats while you down here, right?"

"Yeah!" I looked up from my phone and looked out the window for a minute. My father had set up a meeting with some niggas who were trying to get on. They had been reaching out, so since I was in town, he wanted me to see how much they were talking in regards to money. Niggas talked a good game until money was involved.

"Shoot them a text and tell them to meet me at the warehouse off Dade." He gave me a slight nod and continued to drive.

"You look good, girl!" Looking myself over in the mirror, I couldn't help but smile at how beautiful my cousin had me looking. Without trouble, she was the best, and if I wore makeup every day, I would have her right beside me wherever I went.

"Thanks, boo," I said as I handed her a stack of money, thanking her. After we said our goodbyes, I quickly left. I had a big gift for Diamond, and I wanted to be sure I gave it to her before she walked down the aisle.

It took us about fifteen minutes to get to the church. The line to get inside was wrapped around the building. There were so many familiar faces and, of course, some I didn't know. But just like back in the days, I got out the truck and walked right past them. I heard a few whispers, and even saw a few people roll their eyes, but exactly what did they think? Breeze would never stay down for long.

I walked past everyone with my floor-length mink on, and went into the church, taking a seat on the first bench. I wasn't seated long before an older lady approached me, saying Diamond wanted to see me.

Once I got to the back where she was, I could've cried; my friend was so beautiful. There was a time where it was just the two of us, and just like me, Diamond had no one. Both her mother and father had left her to chase a high. My grandmother took her in until she met Dro, and she moved with him. Dro had money, but from what had been telling me lately, their supply was garbage.

"I know you ain't getting cold feet already," I said, staring at her with tears threatening to fall.

"Friend, I was so happy when I peeped out and saw you. If you want, you can march in the wedding with what you're wearing. I mean, bitch, you rocking the fuck out that mink." I laughed at her and looked down at myself. I looked good.

Though Diamond and I had stayed in touch, she still didn't know my father was a kingpin, and I was basically next in line. I wouldn't say I was hiding it from her, but more so protecting her. She wasn't built for the things I did.

"But on some real shit, I just wanted you to know that Lou is in the wedding, and his girlfriend is most likely here with him." Lou was a name I hadn't heard in years. He was a part of the reason I had gotten the fuck from around here.

"Girl, it's been seven years. Whatever we had is dead and gone. Louis has nothing to say to me, and I have nothing to say to him," I replied, giving her the bag that held one hundred thousand dollars. I wanted my friend to ball out or something once this wedding was over. I never did like Dro, but hey, if she liked it, then I loved it.

I walked out of the dressing room after giving Diamond her gift and proceeded into the church. Imagine my face when I walked out, and Lou walked in with one of Diamond's bridesmaids. We made eye contact and, for a moment, it felt like it was just the two of us in the church. I hated him for the way he always made me feel. I blinked and turned my head. The whole time the ceremony was going on, he looked at me.

I can't wait until I have this meeting tomorrow and head back to Atlanta, I thought.

THREE
LOU

A room full of people, my girl included, and Breeze was the most beautiful woman I had ever seen. But she wasn't the same Breeze. Everything about her screamed *boss*, from the Gucci dress she wore down to the Giuseppe shoes she wore on her feet. She had most definitely glowed up. When she stood up, I noticed the tattoo that covered her entire right leg. I didn't know what it was, but I was intrigued and wanted to get to know this girl, but I knew she wouldn't speak to me.

"Got word back from Lorez?" my homie Dro asked me. This was supposed to be his wedding day, but he was worried about whether Lorez had hit us back up or not. Hell, we both needed the money since our stash houses were hit, and everything in it had come up missing. All we had to our name were two bricks and one hundred thousand dollars. Still, to this day, we had no clue who had run in our shit, but I kept my ears to the streets. Niggas weren't fucking with our product, though, and that was why I felt the need to hit Lorez up. I could no longer deal with the Jamaicans, and word around town was, Lorez was the man to go through.

"Yeah, he hit me back and said he had sent his business partner down here to hear us out. We will meet him tomorrow at the warehouse off Dade," I replied, right before I told him to finish enjoying his reception. Dro and Diamond had been together since they were kids, so I admired their relationship.

The whole time Breeze and I were in the room, we didn't say one word to each other. A few glances here and there, but nothing out of the ordinary. We had been friends for so long, and I know I had hurt her, but her not having holla for a nigga after being gone for so many years was a bitter bitch trait.

I couldn't think about how she was acting right now, though. I had too much going on, and she always knew how to throw me off my game. I was focused on getting to the money. I had been trying to reach out to Lorez for so long, and he had finally decided to meet up. I just hoped like hell he accepted my offer.

"You've been looking at her all night. She's a beauty, isn't she? Even prettier than the pictures I've seen," my girl Joilee said, bringing me from my thoughts.

"I ain't thinking about that girl. My mind was somewhere else."

"Yeah, well, how about you take me over there to meet her. I can finally put a face to all the crazy stories I've heard." I didn't say anything to her, I just grabbed her hand, and we took off, walking in the direction Diamond and Breeze stood.

I knew Diamond's big mouth ass had said something because, after she opened her mouth, Breeze looked in my direction. For the first time tonight, I noticed her face held no emotion. The Breeze I once knew was always happy to see me, no matter what I had done her. She was always so joyful when I stepped in the room.

"Congrats, li'l sis!" I said, giving Diamond a hug, and Joilee followed.

"Hey, Breeze, this my girl, Joilee. I just wanted to come over and speak since we hadn't seen each other in years." I looked to Bre, waiting for her to reply, or at least shake my girl's hand. Instead, she looked at Diamond and continued their conversation.

"Damn, Breeze, that was rude as fuck. I see your attitude still the same." Instead of her arguing back, she grabbed her purse and walked away. I most definitely wasn't used to this Breeze, but I was about to go put her in her place.

"That was awkward!"

"You couldn't have thought it would be anything more than awkward when the two of you haven't spoken to each other in years," Diamond said before walking away.

I looked around until I spotted Bre by the bar. I had to address her disrespectful ass today. I didn't care how long it had been, she would still show me the same respect she had shown me all those years ago.

"Damn, Breeze, that was disrespectful how you handled me and my girl earlier," I said as soon as I approached her.

"It was disrespectful to who, may I ask, because I had no intentions of being disrespectful. I just don't want you to come into my personal space, bringing people with you like I fuck with you or something."

"You really bugging. The fuck is your problem? You don't even know her like that. I know you not still holding on to what we had in the past. That shit was damn near eight years ago, get over it already."

She burst out into laughter like something was funny. "Baby, I am over it, and you. Don't get me wrong, the shit stung me back then, but once you said fuck it, I said fuck the bond. You couldn't have left at a better time in my life.

"Now, if you don't mind, I am trying to enjoy my best friend's wedding, not stand in your face, discussing something that happened years ago." She grabbed her drink and purse and left me standing by the bar, deep in thought. I didn't know what had come over Breeze, but little mama had bossed the fuck up. It kind of made me feel some type of way but turned me on at the same time.

I noticed her as she hugged Diamond and grabbed the rest of her things as she got ready to leave. I didn't know what had come over me, but a part of me wanted to see what kind of car she drove. I wanted to see how she was living, but seeing her get in the back of an all-black Maybach had my mind wandering.

I didn't see a ring on her finger, so I know she wasn't married. But I knew no job had her that decked out. Little mama must be dating a drug dealer or something, and I wasn't talking about an ordinary one. I'm talking about a kingpin; somebody who doesn't touch corners or come out. But once I got on, she'd be crying to come back to me like she always had.

"MAN, what the fuck taking this nigga so long?"

We had been waiting damn near thirty minutes for Lorez's business partner to arrive. This man hadn't texted or called saying he would be running late, but I guess I couldn't complain much. I mean, we really didn't have much choice but to wait or leave empty-handed.

"Sorry I'm late."

I looked up to see Breeze walking our way, and could've shit a brick. Breeze was still one of the finest women I had ever laid eyes on. She was about 5'3, caramel complexion, a few visible tattoos, and her hair flowed down her back, stopping right at the top of her perfectly round ass. The girl had enough ass and hips to help a man survive for days. Her teeth were perfectly straight and white, and in the all-black pants she wore, you could see how fat her pussy was. The bitch was all around bad with a flat stomach and fat ass to match.

"I had a situation come up."

I was so confused when she sat at the table, and looking at Dro, I could tell he was confused as well. I knew Breeze had always had low self-esteem, but I didn't know her shit was so damn low, she had chosen to start dealing with old men. I was so happy I had stopped dealing with her tore up ass. She would never be woman enough for me.

"So, this explains the hundred thousand you gave Diamond last night." I didn't know about that, and I wondered where the rest of the money had come from. I thought he was on some snake shit; Bro had me under eyeing him for a minute.

"I don't mix my business life with my personal life," was all she had to offer. "Now, let's get down to what we are here for. My father said you wanted to cop a few bricks."

Wait, Breeze was this nigga Lorez's daughter? So the bitch was actually a boss. I was most definitely screwed. I'd just let Dro talk to her because she would fuck around and not supply us because she was so hurt behind me breaking her heart.

"Yeah, that's right, but in the bag, I only have two hundred."

"OK, you short eighty, but since I was already coming to offer you a job, I'll just take what you got and front you an extra brick on the strength of Diamond."

"Cool, but what job are you offering?" Dro asked, and just like him, I waited for a response.

"Well, it's simple. I'm opening up shop down here, but I refuse to move back down here, so I want you to run them for me. Every month, I will come get my money, but don't fuck up, because I pop up anytime, without warning. Sixty percent of everything you get goes to me." Breeze had my dick on hard the way she spoke.

"Are you only offering the job to me?" Dro asked, looking from me to Breeze.

"Shid, I was only offering it to you, but if you decide to put him on, then that's you. However, it's still the same. I will be down to collect my sixty percent every month. I opened up five stash houses, and you're over them all. Playing with my money is like spitting in my food, so please, I beg that you and your friend to the left of you don't make me an enemy. I will kill whoever and whatever gets in my way, so don't think I'll spare your life because of Diamond." I had to look at her like she was crazy. This bitch had so much venom in her voice as she spoke.

"You'll knock ya day one off, huh?" I spoke, looking her straight in her eyes.

"My day one said fuck me, so it's fuck my day one, too. Dro, I'll have Relle come in and bring you those bricks, and he'll get the money from you. Don't fuck this up because I won't hesitate to show you I am not the bitch to be played with," she said as she got up and headed towards the door. As quickly as she had come in, she was gone.

"I can't believe we are dealing with her bitter ass," I said to Dro.

"I don't think she's bitter, I think she's hurt. As your homie since kids, the way you played her when we were kids was kind of fucked up. She held it down for you, and you played her over and over again." I was about to reply until the door opened, and a big nigga entered with our supply. Dro gave him the money, and just like that, we were back on.

I wasn't about to apologize to her ass because I had done nothing wrong. I had told Breeze repeatedly to watch the company she kept. She was hard headed, so she went without. I didn't care how much of a boss she was; no nigga was going to deal with a messy, loud, and aggravating-ass woman. Her heart was pure, but we weren't right for each other.

FOUR
DIAMOND

"So, what you gon' do?" I asked Breeze as we sat in the backseat of her Maybach. I was talking her into moving back home, but she wasn't having it. Seven years was enough for her to get her mind together. I needed my friend by my side right now. I had dealt with a lot this last year, but every time she called, I forced a smile and made it seem like things were all right.

"Look, Diamond, how about you roll to Atlanta with me for the rest of this week, and while we are there, I will think about coming back home."

"I don't know, friend, I just got married. Leaving to Atlanta right now wouldn't be a good idea," I said without wanting to tell her my real reason. I feared leaving Dro behind. I knew he was doing something, but I couldn't quite put my fingers on it.

"Diamond, nobody forced a gun to your head when you married that clown-ass nigga. How many times did you catch him back then? What would make you think he changed his way?"

It was like she had read my mind or something, but instead of saying anything back, I shot Dro a text, letting him know I was going to Atlanta. Surprisingly, he responded quickly, giving permission to proceed. A part of me wanted him to ask questions or even beg me to stay, but that was too much like being faithful.

"I can't believe I'm leaving without packing a bag or anything."

"I gave you a hundred thousand, ball out," she said without looking up from her phone. I chose not to respond. I had given that money to Dro so he could come up. I knew it might seem crazy, but we were a team.

"I know you gave that money to Dro; it's in the trunk," she said as she looked up and smirked.

See, Breeze was a friend every girl needed, but she wasn't friendly at all, so I was her only friend. I couldn't help but think about how nonchalant Dro had been earlier when I texted him, but I wouldn't think about that right now.

I wanted to know how Bre knew I had given Dro that money, or more importantly, how she had gotten it back. But as long as everyone was safe, I would stay out of the mix until they let me in.

"I see the way you looking at me, Di, and I know what you are thinking. Don't worry, though, everything is going to be good. I will make sure Dro is good, and I won't let anything happen to you. But, Diamond, just stay out the way and protect yourself at all times. Never hesitate when you are in a situation. This game we are in is very dangerous. Don't trust nobody out here. I promise I'll never cross you, but at all times, trust your gut. If you feel something is not right, fall back."

"Bre, I feel like Dro—"

"Trust your gut feeling," she said without looking up from her phone. We pulled up to her private jet, and at that very moment, I knew my friend was no longer ordinary. My friend was a boss, and she was different than most chicks.

DAMN, I thought as I walked around Breeze's loft, looking at all of her pictures and paintings. Everything was all white, so I knew the thought of her having kids was out the window.

"Bre, you ever thought about having kids?" I continued walking around, waiting for her to answer as I ran across a picture of her, Dro, Lou, and myself. I smiled and wiped it off with my shirt, placing it back on the fireplace.

"When I was younger, I had dreams of getting married and having kids, but it was all a fairytale. As I got older, I knew I might never find my prince charming." I chose not to answer because I knew that once she lost Lou, everything she had dreamed of was now a nightmare to her.

"Who is this?" I asked, pointing to the picture that sat on the corner with her and some fine, chocolate man.

"Girl, that's my ex, Joc. Matter fact, let me throw that picture away right now. He is still a pain in my ass. That nigga a hoe, and very jealous, but his day is coming."

"Check this out. I thought about what you asked me on the flight here, and I hit my realtor up. She found me a nice five bedroom, four bathroom house with a swimming pool and shit. I told her to get the paperwork done, so when we get back, I have to sign the paperwork. I will give it a year, but if I ain't feeling it, I'm leaving.

"Call Keesh to put a welcome home party together, and tell her to pay Young Boy, Joka, and Nipsey to perform. I want Tokyo to host it, and book Club Lemon. There's no budget, just tell her to make sure my shit straight." Keesh was our homegirl from back in the day. She wasn't as cool as Breeze and I were, but she was a fool with the décor. She had been that way since we were kids, though.

"Everything all set, but I ain't yo assistant, bitch." We laughed in unison and continued to run it like back in the day. We talked on the phone every day, but it was crazy how much we had skipped over. These days, Breeze was always so busy, so to have my friend moving back home was a joyous moment for me.

FIVE
DRO

"Shit, baby, I miss this dick," Candy's ass said as I had her bent over, breaking her back.

I know what y'all thinking. Yeah, a nigga just got married, but Candy wasn't anything new, and outside of Diamond, she was the only other female I dealt with. I didn't know what it was about Candy, or what hold she had on me, but I couldn't let her go. Maybe it was the fact she had given me my first son. Diamond knew nothing about Jr., and I planned to keep it that way. I refused to lose her, especially since I was working for her best friend. Breeze didn't pump an ounce of fear into my heart, but I wasn't crazy. She was where the bread was so I would be stupid to make her an enemy.

"SHHHHH!" I blurted out as I released my soldiers into her and rolled over, allowing her to get up and grab me a washcloth.

"I still can't believe you actually married that bitch. I guess it's fuck the fact that I had your first child. I mean, you've been staying over here damn near every night since the wedding, so am I not supposed to be falling more and more for you each day?" Candy was pretty as fuck and reminded me so much of Alexis Sky. The bitch was bad, and a damn good mother, but she was ghetto as fuck, and I couldn't have a loud mouth woman on my arms. Diamond, on the other hand, was innocent and reserved. She was the woman I would want to take out in public. I loved Diamond to my core, but I would be lying if I said I didn't love Candy just the same.

"She don't love you like I do, Dro. She won't ride for you the way I will. I'm telling you she won't," she screamed in between tears. My intentions were never to hurt Candy, and as many times as I had tried letting go, I couldn't. The girl was addictive, and she knew more about me than my own wife. A scorned woman would do anything to see you hurt, so I chose to keep her around, rather than killing the mother of my child.

"Fuck it, I'll just tell her everything the two of us got going on. Either that or I'm putting you on child support. I'm not about to keep playing second to a bitch that don't even look better than me on my worst day." Before I knew it, I had reached out and grabbed Candy by her throat. I didn't care how dirty I did Diamond, no bitch was about to talk about her. Besides, little mama was tripping; Diamond was a candy over her. Diamond reminded me so much of Lauren London, and she dressed her ass off. She had enough ass to sit a cup on top of, and her breasts were small but big enough to grab.

"Fuck you, Dro. I'ma tell that bitch everything!" I could've killed Candy right then and there, but I knew the bitch wouldn't say anything, so for now, I'd let her live.

I had to get home, though, because I hadn't stepped foot in our house since Diamond had left, and she was due to come home tomorrow. I smelled just like Candy's ass, so I needed to wash every part of my body, and my clothes, too.

Pulling up to the house, I noticed the bedroom light on, so I knew she had made it back home.

"Fuck," I said as I walked through the front door and heard her playing Mary J. Blige's "Not Gon Cry". I already knew this was about to be a long night because she only played this song when something was bothering her.

When I walked to the room, she was sitting on the bed, folding clothes. I could tell from her puffy eyes she had been crying, and as bad as I wanted to reach out and touch her, it was best I stayed away. Besides, I smelled too much like Candy for me to comfort her right now.

Standing under the showerhead, I couldn't help but think about everything Di and I had been through over the years. This girl had been with me when I didn't have shit; she literally held me down. Some nights, she stood on the block with me, even when I told her to go home. I knew I was doing her wrong, but I could no longer hide my son from her. Jr. was my world, and because of him, my hustle got deadly, and for that alone, I was no longer hiding him from the world.

Once I got out of the shower and walked into the room, Diamond was fast asleep. The lights and music were off. I knew she didn't want to talk about it, so I climbed in bed and turned my back to her. It didn't make sense for me to hold her tonight, even though I knew I should. I also knew how bad she was hurting.

The next morning, I woke up and rolled over to see that Diamond was already gone. I made a mental note to make sure we talked about whatever was bothering her, but that could wait until later because Breeze was throwing a party tonight, and a nigga had to find something to wear. Every boss in the city was going to be out.

I shot Diamond a text, letting her know I was gone and would talk to her later. To see that she had read all my messages and hadn't replied kind of made me feel some type of way. But I had brought it on myself. Diamond acted so much like a nigga in situations like this, and that was part of the problem.

"Damn, this bitch popping," I said to Lou as we walked through Club Lemon, making our way to the VIP section. I didn't know how this night would turn out, being that Lou had brought his girl with him, but if he said things were cool between him and Breeze, I wouldn't get in the middle of that. Those two were deadly, and that was why they could never be together.

When we reached the VIP, I noticed how laid back Breeze was compared to the loud, over the top Breeze we once knew. She was sitting down, talking with that nigga Relle while Diamond sat to the right of her. Niggas were standing around her, getting lap dances and turning up. Looking at Diamond, I didn't know what I was thinking. My girl looked good as fuck in her Fendi sweater, black, leather shorts, and Fendi boots to match. She got up and greeted me with a hug, walking over and doing the same to both Lou and Joilee. Breeze, on the other hand, only acknowledged me, and even brought me a bottle. Lou as his girl were invisible. She dismissed Relle and moved over, giving me room to sit down on the couch beside my wife and enjoy the rest of the night.

"No, you can sit up here and act like everything good, but I'm going to check this bitch and see if she got a problem." It was obvious both Diamond and Breeze had heard what Joilee said because they both looked in her direction at the same time.

"Man, get that girl," I said to Lou, who was obviously not concerned about what was going on.

"She's a big girl, and she can handle herself. I told her to stand down time after time." That nigga went back to drinking as if everything was good.

"You got a problem with me? Because you been acting real funny since we first met." Breeze threw her hands up as Joilee walked closer to her, and I knew it was to tell her men to stand down.

"Girl, I don't even know you for me to have a problem with you. I'm not friendly, so, therefore, I don't fuck with you," Breeze said as she stood up with Diamond following her. "Now, before things get bad, move around."

"Girl, you may scare these people around you, or even have them fooled, but you don't pump fear through Joilee. Now, show me you really bad so I can bump you down."

"What the fuck going on up here?" Hearing Candy's voice, and seeing the evil grin she wore, had me ready to get the fuck up out the section and go home. I hoped and prayed this ditzy ass bitch didn't say shit.

"Nothing, sus, just handling these hoes and showing them they ain't as tough as they claim," Joilee said as she and Candy stood side by side. I didn't know what the fuck was going on, but I was damn sure about to leave.

"Man, this too much, I'm about to bounce!" Breeze walked past the two of them, but not before Joilee grabbed her by her arm, getting in her face. I wish she had never done that because Breeze turned around and punched her so hard, knocking her down to her knees. Before Candy could jump in, Diamond was on her ass, punching her around the section.

"Damn, baby daddy, so you just gon' let your wife handle me like that," Candy said, which caused Diamond to back away from Candy and look at me with so much hurt in her eyes. I wanted to hug her and explain everything, but she ran out of the section before I could register what had just happened.

"I been told Diamond to leave your dog ass, but she just had to stay. Both of y'all some snake-ass niggas and deserve to be friends," Breeze said as she grabbed her bag off the table and pulled out her gun, shooting both Candy and Joilee. "Clean this shit up while I go check on my friend, and tell y'all girlfriends the next time, I'll aim to kill." Breeze walked out of the club with everyone following her, and not one time did she look back or even show any remorse.

"When the fuck did she become so ruthless?"

I didn't even answer Lou, I just grabbed Candy and helped her heavy ass out the club. Breeze had sent a bullet to her leg, so I was trying my hardest to get this bitch to the nearest hospital before she passed out on my ass. This bitch had caught a bullet and gotten beat up in the same night, but I knew I had taken the biggest loss.

SIX
BREEZE

"Stop fucking crying," I said, screaming at Diamond. She had been crying since we'd left the club. I knew I was being harsh, and I didn't mean to be, but I was frustrated that bitches thought they could come into my section and start drama. Not only that, but I could've sworn I had seen Joc in the club. I couldn't understand his reasoning for wanting to knock me off my throne, but I didn't mind going to war with him. If he thought he would follow me down here and take my spot, he had a lot of niggas to go through.

"I told you to trust your gut feeling. You didn't have to marry that nigga. You act like someone held a gun to your head."

"Whatever happened to my loving and caring friend?"

"I'm still her, but look at the reality of things, Diamond. The nigga had been showing his ass to you. You rather I feed you bullshit, or feed you the truth? If you want to fix your relationship, I'll be here to support you, and if you want to walk away, I'll still be here to support you. But you gotta know that he showed you all the signs, you were just too blind to see them." I felt bad for my friend because I knew how it felt to have your heart broken. "Relle, take Diamond in the house and make sure she don't want for nothing," I said as I got out the car with them and jumped straight into my Range Rover.

Me: Meet me at the warehouse in an hour. You and Louis!

Dro: Bet.

I was mad as fuck, and somebody was about to explain to me why the fuck those bitches felt the need to disrespect me. Nothing had changed with Louis. Just like back in the day, he always felt the need to pillow talk about me to the next female. It was crazy how a female I knew nothing about, decided to come at my neck because I refused to befriend her. But if her man had told her so much about me, then she should've known I wasn't friendly.

"What the fuck was that about?" I asked as soon as I walked into the warehouse. I was pissed off about how things had gone down. I looked at Dro and Lou, waiting for them to answer me when I noticed they were still covered in blood.

"I fucked up bad, and before you think something was set up, I didn't tell Candy to come down to the club."

"I never thought it was a setup, but I'm feeling like it now. Look, both of you put me in a bad situation when those females stepped in my section. I already have a nigga out here on my head, and the mistake that happened back at the club could cause me to ruin everything my father worked so hard to build."

"Bre, let me holla at you for a quick second!" Louis said, causing me to roll my eyes. I wasn't in the mood to fuss with anybody tonight, but I decided to dismiss Dro so he could go talk to Diamond.

"Make it quick!"

"Man, when the fuck did you become so ruthless?" I was about to answer Lou, but I stepped back and took his appearance in for a moment. Not one time did he change. He reminded me so much of the model, Tristan Kenneth. His beard was freshly groomed, and the tattoos that covered his neck and arms stood out. He opened his mouth to speak again, his diamond-encrusted grill shining. I think he knew I was staring hard because he licked his juicy lips. If I weren't on a mission to find out what was going on, I would've jumped on him.

"I'm not ruthless, I just don't like drama around me."

"Since when?"

"Since I'm running a billion-dollar empire and niggas are waiting for me to fuck up so they can take over my throne."

"So, who we have beef with?"

"You don't have beef with anybody, this is all me. But it will be handled. It's going to be hell for them or anybody else to get me up out here," I truthfully spoke.

"You know, Breeze, you don't always have to be so hard. Let me help with this. At the end of the day, you are bitter about some shit that happened between us damn near eight years ago. You claim you've moved on, yet every time I see you, the mug you wear on your face gets meaner and meaner."

"Lou, I'm over what happened. You keep bringing that shit up like you're the one worried about it. Back then, you told me I was too trusting, and now since I don't give any fucks, I'm ruthless. My nigga, don't confuse my hustle in the streets with hurt feelings because my days of loving you are dead and gone. I'm just out here trying to make sure you and everyone else eats." He wanted me to be hurt behind what happened, but I was over that, and I needed him to let it go and stop bringing it up every time we crossed paths.

"Stop acting hard and let a nigga protect you!"

"The same way you did my heart?" my contradicting ass asked. "Look, I gotta get up out of here and figure some things out. I got the whole town of White Castle on my payroll, so her telling on me or anything I have going on will have her missing sooner than I intend. Show me how much you really wanna protect me. Show me where your loyalty really lies," I said right before I walked out the warehouse. I had to get far away from this man before I fell back into his trap.

My mind was everywhere after leaving the meeting with Lou, so instead of going home, I decided to take a nice ride through the city.

Things were going so well, and after that last encounter I had with Joc, I knew it wouldn't be long before he came back around, wanting revenge. But he had no right. He had played himself and thought he could play with me.

Lou, on the other hand, he had done me bad, and for that alone, I could no longer fuck with him. I had learned to let the past be what it was, but truthfully, deep down, the things he had done to me or even said about me had me questioning everything about us. That was part of the reason I didn't want to bring him on, but from the looks of it, Dro was the real problem. After what had happened at the club, I had to watch him, because if he had snaked out his rider for some pussy, he would play with my money. Playing with my money was always a slap to the face.

It was going on six in the morning, and I was riding around, smoking a blunt. My mind was everywhere, and for the life of me, I couldn't think straight. I was running around, playing Russian roulette with my life when all I wanted was to be a stay-at-home wife and raise some bad-ass kids. I never wanted this life. Even though I was damn good at what I was doing, this was not the life I wanted. Being back in my old stomping ground had sure as hell brought back a few memories. Some good, and some bad, but the good sure as hell outweighed it all.

I tried my hardest to get away from the drama, and it was crazy how trouble always followed me. I never said anything, but the real reason I hadn't stayed in Atlanta was because Joc's bitch ass felt the need to try and come for me. I didn't want shit to get too hot, so I decided to move and go back when things died down, or when that nigga died. Either was fine with me, though.

POW!

POW!

POW!

I was so deep in thought, I hadn't seen anybody following me. As I went to reach for my gun, the pain in my side was unbearable. Whoever had shot at me, their day was coming, but as fast as the blood was pouring out of my body, it was best I got myself to the hospital.

I flew through red lights and almost crashed at least twice, but I made it there. I jumped out and ran inside, crashing to the floor. Seeing my mother's smile was what made me realize maybe it wasn't as bad as I thought it was.

SEVEN
LOU

"Who the fuck shot my baby?" I looked up to see Breeze's dad, Lorez, walking through the doors. This was the first time I had seen him, that was how untouchable he was. I could tell Bre being shot had brought out his softer side.

I watched as Relle got up and went to speak with Lorez. It was crazy how one minute you could hate somebody until death knocked at your front door. I sat back, rubbing Diamond's back, trying to get her to calm down. Her ass had been crying since she'd walked through the door. I understood she was hurting, but she needed to remain strong. No one knew Breeze's current status.

"Damn, this has been a crazy-ass twenty-four hours," I mumbled, just as I saw Lorez and some nigga going at it.

"Who is that?"

"That's Breeze's ex-boyfriend, Joc, and from some of the shit she's told me about him, I wouldn't be surprised if he had something to do with this."

"Get him the fuck out of here before I blow this whole fucking hospital up!"

"You ain't got no pull like that, Pops, but no need to cause a scene. Tell Breeze shake back, and I'll see her around," he said before he dropped roses on the floor.

I didn't know why I had taken that as a threat towards Breeze, but I jumped up from where I was sitting and charged at homie, knocking him clean the fuck out. I knew this nigga had something to do with what had happened, and for him to show his face around here, was the ultimate disrespect. This shit was about to get worse before it got better, and I was trying everything in my power to help Breeze's ass, but she kept pushing me away.

"Family of Breeze McGuy."

"Yes, I'm her father!" Lorez said, standing front and center.

"We were able to remove the bullet, but being that she drove herself to the hospital, she lost a lot of blood. We were able to give her a blood transfusion and sedate her. She'll pull through, but we put her in a medical coma until the pain subsides."

"Thanks, Doc. When can we see her?" Lorez asked.

"I know you want to go see her now, but under the circumstances, I'd much rather her body rest tonight, and you can come back tomorrow. She's a very strong girl. With the amount of blood she lost, it could have killed her," the doctor said before walking away.

"Diamond, I don't care what he said, go up there and stay with my baby. The rest of you can go home. Until Breeze shakes back, I'm here to stay, and I'll be who all of you report to. The day she came down here, I gave Relle one job, and that was to stand by her side at all times. Somebody hit my child, so that means somebody violated and forgot who the fuck I am."

I could see where Breeze got her cocky-ass attitude from. She and her dad operated the same way: stubborn as fuck. He didn't even acknowledge the fact that I had knocked a nigga out for him. I wouldn't even trip on that right now, though. I needed to catch up with Joilee and holla at her about something. That was my main reason for coming here until I walked in the lobby and saw Diamond in the corner, crying.

"Hey, 'bout time you came to check on me, being that it's your fault I'm in here," she said as soon as I walked through the door.

"How is it my fault when I told you don't fuck with that? You just had to jump in her face and play like you were bad."

"I don't want to hear that shit, Louis. You are always protecting her. But for the life of me, I don't understand why, especially since she don't show your ass any attention."

"I owe her!"

"Why? Because of the way you did her when y'all were younger? You don't owe her a damn thing. You said yourself you stopped fucking with her because of how loud and ghetto she was. Now since she came around with money and running things, you feel you owe her. Man, you have never been loyal to that girl, so why start now? Breeze bleeds just like the rest of us." It was crazy how I was hurting my girl by protecting Breeze, but let's be honest; how could I ever stop thinking about her when all Joilee did was bring her name up?

"Every day, I'm reminded about the drama you and your childhood fling went through. The portrait of her face on your chest, the many pictures you hold on to in your top drawer, and the fact that you've never deleted her number out of your phone. No matter how many phones you get, you transfer it over, and I'm quite sure she's had a thousand numbers since then," she said through tears. "But you know what's even crazier? While I'm up here suffering from a bullet she sent my way, you were in the lobby with her family. But don't trip, tell her I have just as much pull as her, so you gotta choose a side. It's either Breeze or me." I cocked my head to the side because I knew it was her who had gotten Breeze hit up. I'd play along for now, but I was killing Joilee and Candy as soon as I could.

"Yeah, I'm riding with you," I said as I got in the bed with her. She laid her head on my chest, and I kissed her forehead as I started to put my plan in motion. Dro had better hope like hell Diamond took him back because he was about to be a single father.

Two months later

Thank Allah Breeze had pulled through, and against doctor's

orders, she was back grinding like never before. She and I were doing well on the business side since she'd heard about Joilee's and Candy's sudden deaths. Lorez decided to stay in White Castle until he found out who had shot Breeze's car up. I knew Breeze had a feeling who it was, and I was sure we were all thinking the same thing, but she never brought it up; she just told everyone it was something she had to handle on her own. Diamond wasn't fucking with Dro at all, and I could tell it weighed on him because I had to check on all his spots while he was missing in action. He had Jr. to look after now, so it was best if he pulled himself together and got back to work. I decided to stay clear of everyone's drama and focus on the money.

"You heard me, Lou?" my cousin Keesh asked, waving her hands in my face.

"Nah, repeat it!"

"Dawg, it's just like you to ask for advice but not listen. I said Bre is not the same Bre we all knew back then. You my cousin and I love you like a brother, but I gotta be real with you. You handled her as if she wasn't worth shit. Those was the days when she was at her lowest, and you would just slide in late at night, fuck her, then bounce, only to disappear for days at a time. That girl was fighting silent battles of depression, and you didn't even stop to notice the change in her features. She went away to a mental hospital for five days straight and you never even noticed she had disappeared."

"Damn, cuz, who side are you on!"

"Nobody's side. I'm speaking some real shit because you publicly humiliated her and had everyone looking at her like she was crazy. But she wasn't crazy, she was in love with a man that wouldn't even call to see how her day was going. I love you like a brother, but I'm a woman first, and the way you played the game is the reason you're getting treated the way you are."

"Breeze bipolar as fuck, though. One minute, we good, then the next, we not, so don't blame me for dismissing her."

"She's not bipolar, she's hurt, and just like you don't know what to say, neither does she. All it takes is an apology from the heart, but you too stuck in your ways to finally apologize."

"She deal with me because I'm bringing in money, but that's it. Most days, I don't even see Breeze. The days I do, she's always in and out, only hitting me with a head nod while she engages in conversation with everyone else." Considering the fact that I had knocked my girl off for her, she still wasn't fucking with me, and I felt some kind of way.

"Look, I'ma do you a solid. Big Moo coming home next week, and Breeze is throwing her a little welcome home party at the crib. She asked me to decorate for her, so how about you tag along and come as my plus one. If she has something to say, I'll tell her it was my idea to invite you."

Hearing Big Moo was coming home made me look at Keesh out the corner of my eyes. I wanted to holla at Breeze, but not that bad. I couldn't stand Moo's ass, and she couldn't stand me, but one thing for sure, she was riding for Breeze. Right or wrong, her loyalty was never up for question.

"Man, you know I can't stand Moo ass!"

"That was a long time ago, and this may be your only chance to tell Breeze how you feel." I nodded in agreement and decided to go, but I was punching Moo's ass back this time because her big ass hit like a damn man.

EIGHT
BREEZE

Being shot had set me back. I was thankful for Lou and my father holding things down for me, but I was still pissed that somebody had shot me. I knew in my heart it was Joc, but it was crazy how bad this nigga wanted to get at me. He was trying so hard to take over when all he had to do was be humble. There was enough food out here for everyone to eat, but for some reason, he wasn't going to stop until he ate off my plate.

I found out Joilee was related to Joc, which was crazy because I thought I knew all his people. But that explains why she was coming at me so hard. It wasn't behind a man; it was because her brother was pushing her to test me. Bless her soul, though. Even though I was grateful for Louis killing his bitch, it wasn't going to make me fuck with him.

"Welcome home, bitch!" I said as Moo approached where I was standing. Moo was really my cousin, but I treated her more like a sister. Growing up, we did everything together, and I tried hard to get her to move to Atlanta with me, but she wasn't having that, and that was how she got caught up in the drama. She hung around the wrong crowd, and when she was pulled over, drugs were in the car, but everyone pointed the finger at her. She did five years, and all her "friends" went ghost. But that was how life went.

"All right, bitch, enough of that. I'm ready to go knock back a couple shots of Patrón and have a good time. Big Moo is back, and ready to cause hell."

"Moo, I'm not putting you on," I said once we got in the car. "Moneywise, you straight. I got you a house and a car, but you just got out of jail, so you gotta give this street life up."

"How the fuck can you hustle in the streets, but I can't?"

"See, that's where you wrong. I'm not a hustler, I'm the supplier, and I'm behind the scenes. Only time I'm seen is when my money is played with."

"Damn, so you a boss, boss." We both laughed and continued our drive to the house.

"I heard you put Lou on. You sure you want to fuck with that again?"

"It's business, nothing personal!"

"And how long will that last? You know what, never mind that, let's just get this started. I'll mind my business for now, but you know I can't stand that nigga."

Moo had just come home and was pissing me off already, but this was exactly how things had gone down before I moved to Atlanta. She couldn't stand Lou, and he couldn't stand her, but I stayed clear of all that. It was a battle between my nigga and my blood. That was how Moo was, though. She was that cousin who didn't mind knocking somebody's head off if they looked too hard.

Pulling up at the house, we headed inside to greet everyone. Keesh had that bitch laid out, and it didn't even look like my house. Since Moo was busy catching up with everyone, I went to holla at Keesh and thank her. I spotted Lou at the bar by the pool and wanted to go over there since he hadn't been invited, but I decided against it. I hit him with a head nod and went to enjoy being around family and friends.

"It's time y'all had that talk," Di said as she walked over to me. I looked over my shoulder to see Lou looking my way, and quickly turned my head.

"Now is not the time. I don't want anyone to get the wrong idea. I'd rather stay clear of Lou right now. But enough of us, it might be time you spoke with your husband," I said as I nodded towards the entrance where Dro was coming in.

"The fuck is he doing here?"

"He's a man, and you know how they are; always want to show up and try to make you forgive them for everything they put you through."

"Yeah, but we can't be together. This man has told me repeatedly that he wasn't ready for a child, and he went out there and made one on me. Then, to top it off, he hid him from me for two years. I'm sorry, but I'm not taking care of a child that's not mine. To make matters worse, you still allowing this man to work for you."

"I don't mix business with anything going on in my personal life. You a grown-ass woman, and whatever y'all got going on is between you two. I could have been petty and questioned the fact that you were running around town, going on double dates with Lou and Joilee, but instead, I ain't say shit and overlooked the fact that you hid it from me."

I got up from where I was sitting and went into the house without saying another word to Diamond. I needed to holla at Dro for the disappearing act he had pulled, but I decided against it. I would just send it in a text later. Right now, I needed to get away from all these people.

Big crowds were not my thing, so I went into my office and decided to go over some books. Money had been pouring in, but for some reason, I didn't trust that nigga Dro. He moved too funny for me. I hadn't been seeing him around lately, either, so I definitely needed to get up with him to see what was going on with him.

Knock!

Knock!

"Come in," I said, my head still in the books.

"Can I holla at you for a brief minute?" Hearing Lou's voice took me so far back, it made me want to kill him, but I decided to hear him out. It didn't make sense to keep running.

"Yeah, lock the door behind you." The minute he sat down, he stared at me, making me feel uncomfortable. But, I wasn't going to dismiss him. I hoped he would finally apologize for all the hurt he had caused me along the way.

"Look, I know things between us haven't been the same, and it took me years to say this, but I am sorry, Bre. It's like, no matter how many times I tell myself you not the one for me, something always brings me back to you."

"You sure you not apologizing because of my status? Because I remember you calling me broke when I was at my lowest. So, even though I want to forgive you, I don't know if it's genuine. Louis, I'll never forget the last conversation we had. You dissed me because you said you wanted to travel, and I was fine with that, but was I not good enough for you?"

"See, this is why it took me so long to apologize. Just sit back, hear a nigga out, and please stop fighting me on this. It was never my intention to hurt you the way I did. Hell, you been my best friend since we were kids, so seeing you hurt had me hurting. At one time, you were my right-hand man—well, woman—but you surrounded yourself with a bunch of messy bitches, and I told you repeatedly to let them go. Had you listened to me, you would have never went through all that heartache and betrayal.

"You are the prettiest woman I have ever laid eyes on, besides my mother. I always have and always will love you, but you gotta stop fighting me. Man, I'm sorry for everything you went through, and all the obstacles you fought to be with me, but you weren't hurting alone. No matter what I did, where I went, or who I was with, I could never figure out why I felt like something was missing. The day you came back in town for the wedding, it immediately felt like all the pieces had come together."

After hearing him speak, there was so much I felt I needed to say, or wanted to say, but the tears I had been holding back for years began to flow, and just like that, I was back at a crossroad. I didn't want to forgive him because I was scared he would do it again. Nobody but me and those bottles of Vodka knew what I had gone through. My depression had gotten deep, and my fear of being hurt by another man had caused me to become mean as fuck.

He came around the desk, grabbing me out my seat while kissing my tears away. See, this was the Lou I had fallen in love with. He was always so attentive to my needs. Without warning, he kissed my lips, and I welcomed him by accepting his tongue. The mix of weed and Hennessey sent me over the top.

I allowed him to remove my shirt, taking my nipples into his mouth. Gently sucking them, he looked me in my eyes while picking me up and placing me on the desk. Kicking my shoes off, I removed my pants and allowed him to devour my pussy.

Thank God for a fresh wax, I thought.

"Shhh! Fuck, Lou, I'm about to cum," I screamed. It had been so long since I'd had sex, it didn't take any time for my juices to run down my legs, causing my body to jerk.

When he came up, he smirked and wiped his mouth with the back of his hand. Taking his shirt off, my eyes grew like saucers, but I decided not to say anything and just enjoyed the ride. I rested one arm on the desk, and the other around his neck, allowing him to enter me.

"Damn, Bre, this pussy still good as fuck," he said, kissing me all over. I couldn't even speak, so I bit down on his shoulder blade and rode the wave. This nigga's sex was still good after all these years.

"FUUUUCCCCCCKKKKK!" we screamed together as he released in me. I didn't know what was going to happen after this, but I was once again on the rollercoaster ride of love with Louis Dorsey. *This time around, things would go my way,* I thought as I dropped down to my knees and took my nigga's dick into my mouth, sucking him until he was brick hard.

A party was going on outside, and we were fucking like nobody else mattered.

NINE
JOC

The days of Breeze running the streets as if she were a nigga were over and done with. I was old fashion, so I believed in my girl sitting home and raising kids, not doing a man's job or making more money than the man. Well, technically, she only would pull up to meetings if her father couldn't make it.

Imagine how upset I was seeing my girl come into a meeting, dressed in all-white from head to toe, dripping in diamonds. Then, to make matters worse, she cut our supply without showing any emotions towards me being her man. She looked my way, and I could tell she was shocked, but she had yet to say anything.

Her being the Cocaine Queen was different for me. I tried to stay, thinking maybe I would reap the benefits, being that I was her man, but she walked around the house every day like nothing had happened.

She was driving me with her nonchalant attitude, so I got at her, and decided to ask, *"So, Breeze, you just gon' ignore the fact that my homeboys laughing at me? How I'm your man but didn't know you was the Queen of Cocaine?"*

"Princess!"

"What?"

"I'm the Princess of Cocaine. My father is the king, so that makes me a princess. And, to answer your question, I don't care about your little childish-ass homeboys. Had y'all not been coming up short every time the drop was due, maybe my father wouldn't have cut you. You need to be thanking me because it was me that asked him to cut you short; he wanted to cut you off."

"Bitch, I can't believe how much of a snake you are. You knew all this time, and you still played me."

"You played yourself, I didn't play you. The problem is, you aren't ready to take over. You a pretty boy, and this is not your speed. Every Sunday and Wednesday, you were in church; you couldn't even run the one block my father put you on. Them niggas in that house run over you. Hell, you honestly too weak to even stand by my side in the game." Before I knew it, I had slapped Breeze to the floor.

"Well, I didn't expect that. I'm going to let that slide, but please don't make the mistake of making an enemy of me." I looked at her, and for the first time since being with her, I saw a monster instead of a human. Just like that, I knew she had to go.

"Look at Lorez," my little brother and JT said. We had been following and watching Breeze and Lorez since they had left Atlanta.

One day, my sister Joilee called, complaining about her man's ex being back in town. To my luck, the bitch was Breeze, so I paid my sister to cause a scene that night in the club, but she had gotten her ass beat, shot, and killed a month later. The day the police found her body, they couldn't even recognize her. I knew Breeze had something to do with it, and for that alone, I was going to make her suffer.

"That nigga might as well start counting his days." I grabbed my iPhone to take a quick picture of him and pulled out of the parking lot.

Riding through the city, I realized I needed to put my plan in motion quicker to take Lorez out. That family felt untouchable, and I needed Breeze to feel the same amount of pain my mother felt looking at my sister in that casket, or more. Knocking him off would throw Breeze off her game, but I had a plan for her ass, too.

I turned my beat-up Honda around in the middle of the highway and made my way back to where I had last seen Lorez. God must have been on my side, because just as I was pulling in, Lorez walked out the back door of the club I had seen him go in. Both JT and I loaded our guns and sprayed that nigga up. Before his men were able to react, we were long gone. I know Relle's big ass had seen my face, and that was what I wanted.

"Let's see if Breeze can still hold down the throne," I said as I laughed.

TEN
BREEZE

"Call a muthafucking meeting, and call the bitch, NOW." At this point, I was screaming at the top of my lungs, and my nerves were extremely bad.

"Calm down, we gon' handle it!"

"Calm down my ass. Somebody just violated the fuck out of me. I should've stayed my ass in Atlanta, but that wouldn't have worked, either. I told this muthafucker don't make me an enemy, but his ugly ass insists on reaching." I had to gather myself because I was on the verge of crying. Relle had hit me up earlier and said somebody had filled my father's body up with lead. My dad had long ago prepared me for this; he was high up in authority, so somebody always wanted to knock him down. I knew the day would come, but I didn't know the hurt would sting me this bad. That was part of the game. These streets didn't love anybody, so it was best to enjoy your family while you could.

"Man, you know just like I know this ain't come from nobody in town," Louis said, causing me to look his way. We had been together damn near every day since he'd apologized to me. It was kind of weird at first, but I had gotten used to sleeping with him.

"Yeah, I know!" Joc was trying too hard to see me crack. He wasn't as smart as he thought he was, though. I had hired a private investigator and had had an eye on him since the day I came out of my coma. The day he laid his hands on me was the day I cut him and his potnas off, but killing my father was a different story. I placed a twelve million dollar bounty on his head. Yeah, it was steep, but I wanted him just that bad. I was going to make him suffer.

"Bruh, slow the fuck down." I rolled my eyes because Lou was getting on my nerves. He hadn't even done shit to me, but I was that damn mad. Anybody around me could get this smoke right now. I pulled in the parking lot by the warehouse and started beating the steering wheel. This man had violated me in the worst way ever, and whenever I got to him, I was going to make sure he suffered.

When I walked in, most of my soldiers held their heads down, while the others wore a mug. Right now wasn't the time to be down. I wanted this bitch's head, and I meant every word of what I was saying.

"What the fuck I got y'all niggas on payroll for if y'all can't protect what the fuck y'all supposed to be protecting?" I said, looking directly at Big Mike and Big Lem. My father had specifically hired them to be his guard dogs, but those niggas couldn't do shit right. They couldn't even shoot a nigga. Now, I felt like they had something to do with what had happened, so I pulled my gun and put two between their eyes. I could've knocked Relle off, too, but he was too valuable to me.

"Relle, you're dismissed. I'll get with you later." I didn't even look his way, just continued with what I was saying.

"Clean this mess up, and bring me Joc alive," I said before storming out of the warehouse. Now, I was at the point where I wasn't even pissed anymore; I was hurt that a pussy had decided to play with me. This wasn't the first time my father had gotten caught in the crossfire, but it was most certainly the first time someone had won.

"What was that about?" Lou asked.

"I killed them. What's the point of them being on payroll when they can't act fast enough?"

"You wasn't there, so you don't know how that went down. You too fucking hot-headed. You lost your father and decided to kill two niggas on your team instead of handling the nigga your beef with." I heard everything Louis was saying, but I didn't regret what happened, and I didn't want to talk about the shit.

Today wasn't a good day for me. I couldn't wrap my head around everything that was going on. I got in the car with Lou and lit a blunt. The ride home was quiet, but not because I was mad at what he had said, but because I was fucking hurt. My soul hurt. I didn't have my dad long enough, and a nigga had taken him.

"Hey, friend!" Diamond said as she walked into the room. I had been sitting in the dark in my room since we had gotten home, damn near four hours ago. I wanted to be alone, but this bitch wouldn't allow that.

"You know you can talk to me, right? I know you are hurting, and you always hold your feelings in. Just tell me what's the problem. I'm here to listen."

"Honestly, Diamond, my dad prepared me for this day, so him dying was something I knew would come, but this is not what I want. Don't get me wrong, I love the glitz and glam, but I'd rather do all that sitting on y'all side of the fence. I'm so deep in this shit, I couldn't give it up now if I wanted to."

"Bruh, you can fall back and let Louis take care of everything, but you being stubborn with him. Just give him the chance he deserves." I rolled my eyes. Diamond was indeed my best friend, but the bitch was naïve as a muthafucka.

"Well, if you want me to give him another chance, then how about you call Dro and forgive him, and while you at it, ask that nigga where my money at."

"That shit different, Bre."

"Is it really, Di? Explain to me how. Because a baby not involved? My nigga, we speaking on the same nigga that caused me to lose everything. The same nigga that would publicly disrespect me and treat me like an option. So since we older, and for the last month he's been playing house, I'm supposed to let him take over something my father built?" This was why I wanted to be left alone. I wasn't about to keep speaking on Louis. I had forgiven him a long time ago, but he would have always been over the trap houses. I would never allow him to supply cocaine. "Fuck the past. I don't trust the nigga because I was gone for damn near eight years, and not one time did he come looking for me. He didn't give a fuck then, and he don't give a fuck now."

"Bruh, the man got your face tatted on his chest."

"So if a man walked around here with your face on his chest, you would automatically fuck with him again? You weaker than I thought. It's simple; Lou will never be moved up and be a part of my family business. It won't be long before the nigga does the same thing to me."

"Damn, so is that how you really feel about me? I been putting in work to show you I'm better, even knocked my ole lady off for you, and this how you come." Both Diamond and I looked up to see Lou standing at the door. As much as I didn't want him to hear that, it was the truth.

"Look, Lou, I'm sorry you had to hear that, but if we being real, it's the truth. You did some fucked-up shit in the past that won't allow me to look at you the same. And you knocking your girl off for me wasn't to prove your loyalty. You fucked up when you laid in the bed and pillow talked about me, so you killing her was all on you." I knew I had hurt Lou with what I had told him, but fuck it. Now he could finally see how it felt for someone to play with his feelings.

He walked out of the room without saying anything, and I chose not to run behind him. My days of chasing him were long gone.

"Damn! You ain't got no heart. What the fuck happened to you?" Diamond asked.

"The nigga I loved and gave my all to folded on me, and somebody took the only other nigga I had left that treated me like a queen." Instead of replying, she got up and walked out of the room. Right now, I didn't give a fuck about anybody in this house. They could all leave because I really wanted to be left alone.

The Funeral

Lou and I hadn't talked since we had gotten into it the other night back at the house, but he was right by my side today. Even though I meant every single word I had spoken, I appreciated him for being there, especially since this morning I had woken up weak. I had been in the bathroom, throwing up all morning. I wasn't sure if it was my nerves or something I had eaten. Nevertheless, to be on the safe side, I made sure everyone was strapped up, Diamond and Moo included.

No matter how many times I told myself I was ready for this day, I wasn't. Today was the day of the funeral, and everyone was dressed nicely as they represented my father. His soldiers wore all-black with gold bowties.

"You good?" Lou asked as he grabbed my hand. I nodded and took a deep breath before walking into the church. It was packed, and so many stood around in honor of my dad, I was speechless. I walked up to the casket and placed a soft kiss on his cheek before asking the mortician to close his casket. The people at Roscoe had my dad looking nice, but I couldn't stand to sit on the front row and watch him like that. After twenty minutes of being there, I couldn't stand to see anymore. I ran outside, but immediately wished I had stayed where I was.

"Breeze McGuy?" the officer asked as I stood on the steps of the church. There were at least twenty officers. Some kneeled down by their cars with guns drawn, and others stood to the side. Instead of responding, I gave them a smirk and held my hands out in front of me.

"You are under arrest for the murders of Joilee Dennis and Candy Sanders. You are to remain silent." I didn't hear shit else they said after telling me I was under arrest for murder. I heard Diamond and Moo cry but refused to look back. They placed me in the car, and I looked up, noticing Lou standing there with his hand on his head as

I saw a tear escape. Thinking he had set me up was out the window. Once we drove a little further, I saw Joc sitting off to the side with a smirk on his face. I wanted to spazz, but I remained calm and enjoyed the rest of my ride down to the station.

"Come make your call!"

Knowing I had these bitches on my payroll, they sure as hell hadn't taken care of me or made sure I was straight. I had been there for two days before I was able to make a phone call, and I was mad as hell. My lawyer came up, and he had good news. They hadn't found any evidence that I was the one who had murdered those girls. Besides, I was in a coma around that time, but it was still crazy that they wanted me to sit and finish my probation. A few years ago, I had fucked around and caught a weed charge. Since it was my first offense, they placed me on probation for five years.

"I need to see you ASAP," I said as soon as he answered the phone. I could've used my call to call Diamond, or even Lou, but I dialed someone even more important.

Walking back to my cell, all I could think about was the hell that was about to be caused. Joc knew just like I knew he was about to wake up a sleeping beast. There was someone else in line, and forcing his hand would be like playing spades with the Grim Reaper. You will never win, no matter how good you are.

ELEVEN
CUSH

"FUCK!" I screamed as I flew in and out of traffic. My sister had just called me, and of course, I knew this day would come. What she didn't know was I had been in White Castle since I had gotten the call about our dad being killed. I had been keeping an eye on Joc, and today was going to be the day, but my baby needed me so I would catch him another time.

I'll get that nigga soon, I thought.

I'm tripping, let me introduce myself. My name is Cush Keys. Just like Breeze, I came up in the drug game. Only difference is, I had been there since day one. When she first came to the house, we connected, and since that day, she had been my baby, and I had looked out for her.

Breeze was heavy in the dope game, and my dad had taught us both the ropes. However, that wasn't my speed; I was more for killing muthafuckas.

My father was high up in the game because of my aim skills. I had knocked a lot of people off for him to be where he was. After word got out about my assassination skills, people started paying me anywhere from ten to twenty million a head.

It took me about forty minutes to get down to the jailhouse. I couldn't believe the hate people wore on their shoulder, but my baby was coming home. Parking my Bugatti out front, I jumped out and headed towards the door, but not before checking my surroundings.

"Breeze McGuy!" I said to the woman at the front desk.

"Place all your belongings in the basket, and walk through the metal detector." I heard her, but I couldn't get past her thick-ass mustache.

"Right this way." She led me to a room down a long hallway.

"In here, and she'll be in soon."

"Cush!" Breeze screamed as she ran and jumped in my arms. I didn't care how gangster I was, seeing my baby in that orange jumpsuit broke me down, and I felt like I had failed her. I was supposed to protect her from this part of the game.

"The fuck you do?"

"That nigga Joc gotta go. He lied and said I killed two li'l chicks I got in an altercation with a while back."

"Don't trip, li'l sis, his time will come. What did the lawyer say?"

"They couldn't find any evidence on me so they could pin that shit with me, but I'm still not coming home. They want me to sit and finish my probation out for that li'l weed charge I caught."

"How long did you have left?"

"Two and a half years. I'ma knock that down in no time. However, I called you down here because I want you to take my seat until I get out. You the only one I trust, Cush. I know this isn't your speed, but I need you to hold shit down for me."

"You know I got you, li'l sis!"

"Don't speak on my time with anyone because I want to surprise them when I get out. Only you will know everything about what's going on up until my release date."

"Sis, you know I got you, and I'ma double your profits. Don't sweat it. That two gon' go by before you know it, then you coming home," I said, and she immediately began to cry.

"Don't cry, Breeze, I got you!"

"I know, and I'm not crying because of that, I'm crying because I'm pregnant and about to do two years. This is going to be harder on me than I thought."

"Pregnant? Who the fuck is you pregnant for? Did Dad know?"

"Lou," she said sadly, and as bad as I wanted to hold my sister and tell her everything would be all right, I didn't. I just got up and walked away. I'd told her I would hold her down, and I was going to stand on that, but I was pissed that she had gone and gotten pregnant by that nigga Lou.

I didn't know a thing about him, but I knew I had to hold Breeze when she first touched down because he had broken my baby's heart. These days, Breeze was most certainly a boss, but she was a female who still had a heart.

TWELVE
BREEZE
TWO YEARS LATER

I'ma say I'm sorry for all that shit that I had did.
And I'm thankful for all that shit you did when we was kids.

I WAS FLOWING through the streets of Baton Rouge with Cush, listening to Young Boy. Today was my first day out, and as promised, Cush had held court down, making sure to double my profit. He had even taken care of the twins while I was gone. Yes, I had given birth to a boy and a girl, Cane and Cali. Moo and Diamond made sure to write and make sure I was straight, and they even took turns getting my kids for me.

Lou didn't know about the twins, but the way I saw it, he didn't care about them, either. He had come to visit a couple times, but after I told him I didn't know when I was coming home, he stopped answering and got a new girl. I wasn't even mad this time around. Hell, I wasn't even hurt because I had done it to myself.

THOSE YEARS away from everyone was hell, but I sucked it up.

Muthafuckas had left me high and dry, but those who stayed would always get my highest honor. Word around town was, Lou had really come up, but what he didn't know was he was still working for me.

Tonight, Cush was throwing a big-ass party, and since it was my first day out, I decided to attend.

"YOU GOOD?" my brother asked.

"YEAH, I'm straight, bro, just ready to see the look on everyone's faces."

"MUTHAFUCKAS GON' really trip out, but your little plan worked. Lou think you broke. He saw those kids plenty of times, and not one time did he stop and notice they were his." I couldn't help but shake my head at the way Lou had been moving.

"HE REALLY A MARK-ASS NIGGA, SIS."

"WHAT'S UP WITH DRO?"

"DIAMOND DIVORCED HIM. I guess she couldn't get over the fact he had a child on her. She tried, but once I came around and started beating that li'l yoni up, she left him high and dry. Nigga a snake anyway, and I don't trust him."

"UMPH, JUST DON'T HURT HER," was all I had to offer. I already had too much going on so I wouldn't get in their business. But hearing him say Dro was a snake had me thinking hard about everything. I was going to look into that because I found it strange that he had come back around while I was locked up.

I just wanted to get to my kids and kiss all over their chubby cheeks.

"YOU READY?" Relle asked as we pulled up to the party. I had to get my hair and nails done, so I was already damn near two hours late. I was nervous as hell. All these people thought I had a life bid, so imagine the look on their faces when they saw their boss was back.

"YEAH, tell Cush to open the back door of the club." Relle pulled out his phone and did what I had asked.

SINCE HAVING THE TWINS, I had stacked up in all the right areas. I had always had ass, but they had given me more. Tonight, I decided on a Gucci sweater with Fashion Nova jeans and a pair of Gucci tennis. I wasn't for wearing heels on my first day out, and I wanted to finally fit in. I wore my hair up in a messy bun, and makeupbyDaria had slayed my face once again.

"YOU LOOK NICE, LI'L SIS."

I had to admit, my bro had Club Lemon on and popping. It was his birthday, and to say he had only been in the game two and a half years, he had the streets on lock.

Walking in the club, it was like old times, and I was ready to drink and have a good-ass time.

. . .

"OH SHIT, Boss Lady back in the streets, and in the building." I looked up to the DJ and waved as I made my way across the floor.

"I DIDN'T EXPECT THAT," I said to my brother.

"HELL, NEITHER DID I." We made our way to the VIP section, and as I expected, Diamond and Moo were all over me like they hadn't seen me in forever. Well, I guess they hadn't.

I WALKED across the room and hugged all my men as they welcomed me back. When I reached Lou, I hit him with a head nod and went back to talking with my brother, enjoying being a free woman. I didn't expect Lou to completely hold me down. However, I also didn't expect him to turn his back on me. After two months, he stopped answering my calls, and after five months, he had a new woman on his arm. I guessed that was her sitting on his lap, but I could no longer trip. I had set myself up when I fell back in his trap. The only difference was, kids were involved this time.

"WE WILL MEET tomorrow and go over everything. I also need word on Joc, but that can wait until tomorrow."

Looking at my brother and Diamond all on each other while I talked business made me cut everything short and go on to enjoy my night. I sat on the couch and looked around, and I was happy to see all my men were still behind me. It was crazy how I was so deep in the game, I didn't have a love life. Most women would give this up just to be loved, but every time I thought I was going to be loved, something stood in my way.

. . .

"WHEN WERE you going to tell me you was getting out?" Lou asked as he came and sat next to me.

THERE WAS nothing more for us to discuss, so I chose not to answer whatever he had to say. I was ready to give all this up, and what he didn't know was, I was going to pass it down to him. This wasn't Cush's speed, so he didn't want it, either, but I wasn't about to let an outsider run something my daddy had built. So, for now, I'd keep it.

I got up and walked away, going to stand by my brother. It was safe to say Lou and I were back on the same terms. We had run our course, and this time, I was really done.

"HOW YOU GON' handle the situation?" Diamond asked me.

"HONESTLY, Di, I'm not. We've been here how many times? It will all play itself out."

"YEAH, BUT KIDS ARE INVOLVED NOW." I shrugged and walked off. I knew I had kept them from him, but if he hadn't noticed they were his in all this time, he didn't need to know. It was obvious his new chick had him too caught up in whatever they were doing to care.

"YOU TAKING BACK OVER?" she asked as she followed me.

"YEAH!"

. . .

"BITCH, good, because my baby ain't built to be a cocaine cowboy. His ass be tired, tired."

"IT'S obvious you don't know your man then," I said, leaving her in her thoughts.

"I'MA GET up out of here, brother. I'm going to get the kids from May and go home." May was the kids' nanny, and she just didn't know she was moving in with me. From my understanding, Cane and Cali loved her, and she loved them just as much. Though I would be home a lot, I still needed her there with me.

"A'IGHT, sis, I'ma get up with you tomorrow at the warehouse." I hugged Diamond and Moo, making my way out the club.

"DID YOU ENJOY, BOSS?" Relle asked.

"YOU KNOW I'm too lowkey for big crowds, Relle. I'm just happy to be back home, and thank you for holding me down." Relle was another one who constantly wrote me and made it a point to come see me. It had been that way since I'd moved to Atlanta. The first time my father introduced us, we instantly clicked, and just like that, he had always had my back. He was there for my first kill, and always a shoulder. I had so much respect and love for Relle, it was insane.

I had come back to White Castle for Diamond, and a part of me had missed it, but being down here wasn't the same. I was lying, it was the same. Too much of it was the same, and the memories were painful. Lou and I had kids together now, and I had just done a two-and-a-half-year bid. I wanted better for my kids, so I think it was time for me to go. Lou had once again shown me that love didn't love anybody. Moving back to Atlanta wouldn't be so bad, and I knew Cush hated it down here, so I was ready to go back home.

"WELCOME HOME, BOSS!" my li'l soldier Tip said as I walked into the room. Tip was one of my top soldiers; it was crazy how much sauce I saw in the dude. He was young, but the hustle he had was crazy. I gave him a genuine smile and continued to speak with the rest of my men.

"FIRST AND FOREMOST, I want to thank my brother Cush for stepping up and taking over while I did that li'l bid. Next, I want to thank those of you that kept the faith that I was getting out and held me down. Real niggas like you all are rare, so for that, thank you," I said, looking to everyone in the room, except Lou.

"Now that I'm back, my brother will be stepping down, but he will still stand by my side. Every month on the fifteenth, I will be down to collect what's mine. My family and I have decided to move back to Atlanta." I saw the look on Lou's face, but right now, it was fuck that nigga. Shit got real, and that nigga folded on me.

"YO, Bre, let me holla at you," I heard him say.

"NAH, I'm good, I'm handling business," I said as I went on to discuss everything else, making sure shipments were a go. Choosing Cush was a good idea; he had made sure the money continued to come in.

"OK, and before we go, Tip, I heard you really been doing your thing. I want you as head of the trap on Jade Dr. I'll start you off with one, then I may move you up." I watched his face light up like a kid on Christmas morning.

"That's it, y'all dismissed," I said as I turned to finish talking with Cush.

"When were you going to tell me you were moving?"

"She ain't have to tell you shit!" Cush walked up on Lou, but I stood in the middle of them and held my hands up.

"Come on, Lou! Why would I tell you I was leaving?"

"I deserve to know!"

"I deserved your loyalty, but when you thought I was going to be down for a long time, you left. Be cool, and be happy you still on my team."

"Bruh, this shit doesn't mean nothing to me. I thank you for everything you've done, but it's crazy how every time we fall off, you always on that shit, talking about how you put me on."

"You don't think I should remind you? Anybody in their right mind would have watched you suffer. You a hoe-ass nigga, and the fact that you standing in my face, questioning me about fucking moving is beyond me. This is the second time I've needed you, and you basically said fuck me. Not only did you turn your back on me, but my brother was also raising your kids while you were out here, once again, playing house."

"The fuck you mean, raising my kids?" I didn't answer him. I looked up at my brother, who mugged Lou, and grabbed his hand so we could leave. Louis and I were over, and I was tired of crying over him. I was tired of being an option for him. There was nothing in this world I lacked. I had everything, and I refused to let my daughter see a man mistreat me because then, she would think it was normal.

"Breeze!" Hearing Lou call after me tore my heart apart more than it already was, but having Cush push me closer and closer to my car made it all better. Sad as it was, we just really was anyone perfect love story.

THIRTEEN
KOSHA
LOUIS' GIRLFRIEND

The only reason I wanted to meet up with this bitch Breeze was because I saw the way Lou looked at her when she came to the club that night. I had no business reaching out to this woman because she hadn't even spoken to him, but I had heard the many stories, so I had to at least try and pump a little fear through her. I needed her to know my spot with him was solidified, and no bitch was coming after me. I had done more for him in two years than she'd done the whole time they had been together. Just because her face was tatted on his chest didn't mean she still had a place in his heart or our life.

"What's up?" I said as I walked around the table to have a seat across from her. This girl's face held no emotions, and she didn't even bother to speak back. She took her glasses off and looked at me as if she was waiting for me to speak.

"I only called you here to let you know that Lou and I are together now, and whatever y'all have or had is dead," I said before rolling my eyes.

"Does Lou know you reached out to me? Don't even answer that, because I know for a fact he doesn't. Louis don't play behind his precious little Breeze. See, you're threatened by me, but I don't give two fucks about the two of you. I can be dirty and show you pictures and text messages, but I can see right through you. You're a duck. Louis always did go for your kind. He likes a weak bitch that won't leave when all his dirty laundry is aired out. The nigga you love, loves me. I'm the one that chose for us to no longer be together. I'm the one that chose to walk away. That nigga you got ain't nothing but a lying, cheating, deceitful snake with a big dick. So while you in my face, telling me to stay away from a nigga I don't even speak on, make sure you keep that same energy when telling him the same. Next time you reach out to me, make sure you thank me for stepping down from my throne, allowing you to take a temporary seat. My name holds weight in that nigga's heart," she said as she got up and grabbed her things to walk away, but not before saying one more thing. "And make sure you suck and ride my nigga's dick better than me, because, at all times, I left it creamy and made sure to catch all his kids. I never left a mess behind!"

"See, the difference between the two of us is, you caught them with your mouth, and I'll be sure to catch them in my pussy and give him the family you didn't."

"Girl, I've already gave him a boy and a girl. While you tryna be a big, bad wolf, tell him to come over and see his kids. We leave tonight, but he can come meet them if he'd like. Oh, and Kosha, your days are very limited. I'ma teach you a lesson about playing with a bitch that's as high as I am. Tick tock, tick tock!" she said as she backed away from where I was sitting. I had fucked up royally, thinking I could chest up to her. I was no fighter, but shit, I didn't think this meeting would go as badly as it had, either.

"Kids?" I questioned before shooting Lou a text.

ME: So when were you going to tell me about your kids?

HUBBY: Huh? What the fuck you talking about?

ME: Breeze! I just spoke with her and she told me to tell you to come see your kids before they leave tonight.

HUBBY: Tf you doing talking with Breeze? Didn't I tell your looney toon ass to stay the fuck away from her?

I chose not to respond because Breeze was right. Lou did not play behind her, and while I was out here, going crazy over him, I knew in the back of my mind, I was just a fling until Breeze got her shit together. But they would not want to cross me until I was finished securing this bag. If I left, they would both have to pay me off. I didn't know what position Breeze held, but I assumed it was high up after hearing everyone refer to her as Boss.

FOURTEEN
LOUIS

"Stupid bitch!" I said as Breeze ignored my call for the tenth time. I had heard her when she was in the warehouse, ranting, and I had been trying to holla at her about these kids she claimed I had, but this bitch was really on a thousand right now. Then, to add insult to injury, Kosha's dumb ass had decided she wanted to go behind my back and meet up with Breeze. The women in my life were on some other shit right now, but it was time I put my foot down.

I pulled up in Breeze's driveway and walked right up to the front door. I didn't care that Cush, Diamond, or Moo were outside, loading up the U-Haul. She had me fucked up if she thought for a second she was about to hop up and move away.

"Breeze!" I screamed through the house, just as she turned the corner, holding twins in her arms.

"What are you fucking doing here? You need to be checking your bitch about thinking she's going to play with me."

"Fuck whatever y'all got going on. I'm here because you drop this bomb on me that I have kids, then you just decide you gon' take them away without even consulting with me."

"These kids been around, and if you didn't stop to wonder where kids just popped up from, or why they look like you, then you don't care. Now, get the fuck out my way before I air this bitch out."

"Man, you so muthafucking unfit! How are you going to air something out with your kids sitting right there?" I screamed, pointing at the kids who sat on the floor. "Bitch, I will really kill you because you think you can't be touched."

"But where I'ma be when you pull the trigger, li'l brother?" Cush asked from behind me. I was so pissed at Breeze, I hadn't even heard them come in.

"You can get bodied right with her!" I honestly stated. I had kept quiet long enough, and I think that was what made muthafuckas think they could play with me. But I was far from a corner-hustling nigga who needed them. I knew I had hurt Breeze in the past, but we should be over that shit now.

"Bitch, you bitter as fuck, and if you take my kids away from here, once I walk out that door, be ready for a war."

"Is that a threat or a warning?"

"This is between me and my baby mother, and since you asked, it's a promise," I said, mugging Cush.

"I went to war with twenty niggas; you think I'm scared to go to war with one? I'll kill the closet muthafucka to your heart if you think you gon' play with me, Lou."

"You just don't know how bad I wish death upon her right now," I said, speaking of her. I turned to walk out the door because I had nothing left to say. I knew Breeze wouldn't listen to me, but I was about to make a move to Atlanta and show her who was the real boss. I played about a lot, but my family wasn't something I played about. Not only was I pissed because she was taking the kids away, but I wanted her here with me as well. I wanted to get to know my kids and wanted to make her my wife.

"Bitch!" Moo said as she punched me in the back of my head. I was so mad, I turned and punched her ass like she was a man, knocking her down to the ground. But the bitch was so cocky, she got up, and we started fighting. She fought like a nigga, but she wasn't one. Cush jumped in, and to say homey was the pretty boy type, he had a pair of hands on him.

POW!

The gun went off, causing both Cush and myself to look back and see where the sound had come from.

"Next time you come in my house and stir shit up, I'll forget you're the father of my kids and make sure I aim for your head. You come in my house like you fucking Iron Chest Charlie, sending threats my way because you don't want me to move. But not one time did you pick your kids up. Do you even know their names?" I was about to respond, but I chose not to.

"You a mark-ass nigga, Lou, and you been this way since we were younger. You keep saying I'm bitter, but baby, I'm far from that. You showed me your ass, and each time, I accepted you back. But that moment I fell off, or you thought I did, you bounced on me. I fucking needed you, bitch, and you weren't there, so yes, I'm taking my kids, and I'm leaving. Build a family with that bitch, but please, whatever you do, don't start something you can't fucking finish."

Looking at Breeze, I noticed her emotionless eyes were filled with pain.

"Oh, and don't worry about doing business with the Keys family anymore. I'm cutting you off, and before you think this is personal, it's not. The moment you sent a threat my way to start a war, the li'l business I was still giving you was cut off."

"You going too far!" She walked off and left me standing in the foyer, speechless. Good thing I had enough saved up because she had really cut me the fuck off.

"No need to reach out to the Lopez family or the Jamaicans either because Breeze supplies them as well. Think about the consequences if you go behind her back," Cush said and walked out. I didn't say shit to his pussy ass, I just walked out the house.

I didn't care what Breeze and I went through, I wouldn't ever go behind her back that way. I'd just fall back until she calmed down. But, for the first time ever, a female had me in my feelings, and by the balls. The shit Breeze was doing had a nigga hurting, but I wasn't going to trip.

"Bae, I cooked your favorite!" I didn't even know how I had gotten in this situation with Kosha. I had every intention of holding Breeze down, but I couldn't stand seeing her like that. Kosha was just a fling and, without my knowledge, she had moved in. I didn't want her, but shit, she was something to make time fly by.

I didn't know what had come over me, but I walked to the stove where the food was and started throwing all of that shit away. The incident between Breeze and myself was partially my fault, but this stupid bitch had made it worse the moment she decided to call a meeting with the devil.

"Why did you do that?"

"Look, Ko, I appreciate you for everything you've done, but you gotta get the fuck up out of here."

"Damn, you really that mad because I went and met with Breeze? I don't know what's so important about the bitch. She not even all that cute." This bitch just didn't know how much of a turn off she was, saying something like that. Breeze hadn't done a damn thing to her, and honestly, not wanting to fuck with her had nothing to do with Breeze. We had run our course, and I was no longer feeling her. Hell, I was never feeling her.

"You know what, Lou, I'll leave and get out your hair, but not before you give me two million dollars." I had to laugh at the bitch when she said that.

"Bitch, you crazy. You ain't about to get no money up out of me so you can stay, and I'll leave. Matter fact, I had planned to move to Atlanta anyway. I don't know how you gon' pay the bills here, but you can have it."

"What the fuck you mean, you moving? I don't have any money to support myself, Louis." I walked upstairs to pack up everything, emptying my safe. Kosha would find a way to make it, but I was going to get my family back.

I realized something. I didn't care how much pussy I'd had, or how many times I'd tried to make myself believe I didn't want Breeze, it was all a lie. The girl had my heart, hands down, and I made a promise to myself that if I were to get her back this time, I wouldn't let her go.

"You ready?" I said as soon as Tip answered the phone. I had groomed him to be where he was today. So to see Breeze move him up made me feel like a proud father. Now that he was getting more money, he could leave for a few days.

"Yeah, nigga, pick me up from the crib."

When I made it down the stairs, Kosha was on the phone with a huge smile on her face. I knew then I would have a problem with her, but as quickly as I had slid in, I had slid out and was on my way to Atlanta. It was time I finally put my foolish ways aside and do right by my family.

Atlanta, here I come, I thought as I pulled out the yard and hit the road.

TIP

"YOU GOTTA SHOW me you a man since you claiming you are. Show me. Pull your pants down and show me."

"No, mama!"

"Come on, let me see that dick. Let me see if it's as big as your ego."

I was a young boy then, but I still remember that day as if it were yesterday. I was now twenty-five, but I still held so much anger in me from the day my mother forced me to have sex with her. She started when I was ten, and continued until I was eighteen. Eight years of my life ruined, but outside of her, I had no family, and I didn't want to be moved from foster home to foster home, so I just took the abuse silently.

Meeting Breeze when she first moved down here was one of the best things ever. I promised her I would prove my loyalty to her, and I had done just that. There were plenty of times I had stayed up on the block and hustled. I had nowhere to stay or food to eat, so until I came up, everything came last. That was almost three years ago, and now here I was. Don't let my swag fool you, I was still the same ratchet nigga who liked to get down, I just wore Gucci shoes, or whichever I decided to choose.

"What's up, Lou?" I said as I got in the car with him. Louis was one of the only niggas who looked out for me and gave me somewhere to lay my head when I was out here. He said I reminded him so much of himself, and to me, that was a compliment. The nigga was a born hustler and leader, I just hoped him and Breeze could get it together.

"So, what's your plan when we make it?"

"There is none. I know Breeze's tough ass won't be so accepting, but I'm going to try. I can't lose Breeze. Despite what everyone has to say about her, she's a real one, and all that anger came from me hurting her."

"I feel that, big bro, but this time might be your last time, so don't ruin it. You know Boss Lady is tough as fuck when it comes to her feelings, but I got high hopes for y'all."

The rest of the ride to Atlanta involved us smoking and running it about coming up in a major way. I respected and honored Breeze and Lou so much, and if they needed to, I would let them carry me on their taxes. I was old as hell, but I owed them that because, without them, I didn't know where I would be.

"We here, young blood!"

The ride was so damn long, I had gone to sleep. I was high as fuck and honestly hadn't slept in days. Since Breeze had promoted me, I didn't have to stand on corners anymore, but I sat my ass in those trap houses, day in and out. I didn't trust muthafuckas around my money, and that was why I was nervous about taking this ride with Lou.

"This Breeze crib?"

"Yeah, I want you to go in first."

"Wait, how the fuck did you know where she laid her head, though?"

"I have my ways."

"I got a bad feeling about it." Instead of waiting for him to respond, I walked towards the door.

Now, I was a street nigga, so that gut feeling I got had always been on point. I didn't know how this would turn out, but the feeling I had in my stomach told me I should get back in the car. But after constantly knocking with no answer, I took my chances and turned the doorknob. I walked into the house, and to say Boss Lady had just moved back to town, the house was laid out, but she was moving like she didn't have a care in the world. I knew I wasn't tripping, and I knew for a fact I heard moaning. I peeped my head in the first room I saw when I reached the stairs, and the twins were laying in their beds, asleep. The second room I looked in was Breeze's room, and the view I got wasn't pleasant. I knew the betrayal would hurt Lou, so I chose not to say anything.

"Damn!" I heard from behind me, and when I turned around, Lou was standing over my shoulders, looking through the crack of Breeze's room as she and Relle fucked like they didn't have a care in the world.

"Come on, let's get out of here."

"Nah, not before I get my kids. If she wants to be a hoe and fuck the help, then I'll show her better than I can tell her."

"You tripping. You just hurt right now, let's get out of here."

I wasn't going to lie, I felt some kind of way that Breeze was moving the way she was, but they were both hurt. The crazy part was, Lou and I stood in the hallway, having a whole fucking debate about kidnapping his damn kids, and not one time did they stop fucking. After a while, I just said fuck it, grabbed one of the twins, and ran for the door, making sure not to trip over shit and make noise. I had come this far to help him conquer love, not get my head blown off.

"This about to be war between Breeze and every-fucking-body."

It was crazy how life worked, and this was why I refused to be in a relationship. I knew for a fact I couldn't give a woman what she wanted right now, so I wouldn't even try. Breeze wanted Lou, and

Lou wanted her, but the way they were going about everything was going to leave them or somebody around them hurt in the end. I knew for a fact Lou was hurting because, even though he had done everything under the sun to Breeze, she was never supposed to let go.

"We staying in Atlanta, or heading back to town?"

"We gon' stay here for a while and watch her run around like a chicken with her head cut off."

This would not turn out good, and I knew it wouldn't because I'd seen them both in action. I had seen both of them kill without any remorse, but I wouldn't get involved. I had never been to Atlanta before and had enough money to buy a few bitches, so I was about to turn the city the fuck out. They might as well get ready for TIP because before I left and headed back home, I would make sure my name was well known.

FIFTEEN
BREEZE

After sitting back and thinking, I kind of felt bad for the way I had handled the situation with Lou, but a bitch was mad and hurt, once again. I knew I was never supposed to act on my emotions when it came to business, but this damn rollercoaster of love and betrayal we were on was beginning to tear me down. However, my way of getting over the shit was no better than what he had done to me.

"Breeze, I know you might think what we just did was a mistake, but it wasn't."

I didn't even know how I had ended up in this predicament with Relle. One minute, he was helping me set everything up for the twins, and the next, he had me bent the fuck over. I didn't know if I was rolling off emotions, or if it was the fact that I had spent damn near three years away from dick, but I chose not to think too hard and just enjoyed the moment.

I had no intentions of being with him, but if he dropped consistent dick, I wouldn't turn it down. It was far from Lou, but I couldn't complain; he had a good stroke game, and the size was fairly nice.

"I'm going to check on the twins. That's not a conversation I want to get into after we just finished fucking."

"But we will have to talk about where we will go after this soon."

"Damn, after just one time?"

I didn't even wait for him to respond; he was tripping already. I couldn't be with a man if I wasn't fully over the last one.

"WHAT THE FUCK!" I screamed as soon as I walked into the twins' room. I immediately calmed down and went to grab my phone from the nightstand. Maybe Cush and Diamond had grabbed them, or maybe Moo. The nanny wouldn't arrive until tomorrow, so I knew it wasn't her. I also knew no one would violate me on this level. I immediately sent a group text to everyone.

ME: One of y'all came and got the twins?

Diamond: No, Cush and I are at the movies.

Moo: No!

Me: Bruh, my fucking babies are gone. Please tell me one of you are playing a joke on me.

Cush: Tf you mean gone? We leaving the movies right now and on the way over.

Moo: Pulling up now.

I couldn't even focus, and I was mad at myself for not getting those cameras set up before I made it. I had everything laid out in my crib when I got there, but the cameraman was due to install everything the next day. Nobody would dare walk into my home and take my kids, so when my family walked in the door, my kids would be with them. We played pranks on each other all the time when we were kids. They were funny like that. I would be mad at first, but we would laugh about it later.

"Everything good?" Relle asked as he sat beside me, and I was happy to see he was dressed. I didn't have time to explain shit to Cush's ass.

"Bitch, what's going on?" Once I saw Moo walk in without my kids, I started to panic a little more. Of all the bad I'd done, and the people I'd killed, my kids had come along and softened my heart just a little. I would be weak without them.

"Where are my fucking kids?" I screamed just as Cush and Diamond walked in without them.

"Somebody playing with me. What did I do to deserve this?"

"Come on, sis!" I had never seen my brother cry, but seeing me so weak must have brought the tender side out of him.

"The whole fucking city about to feel me for this one."

It had been a whole week since my babies had been gone, and no one knew or had heard anything. I couldn't get the police involved, being that I was running a damn drug empire, but something had to give. I had reached out to Louis a few times, but he refused to pick up the phone for me. I knew he was mad about me cutting him out, but damn, this nigga's kids were missing, and not one time did he think me calling could possibly be important.

"Come on, Breeze, you got to get out this bed."

"I'm not in the mood, Moo."

"I understand that, but you laying in this bed won't bring them back, and that bounty you put on whoever head won't make things easier, either."

"Niggas will do anything for money. I bet my kids be back home by the end of next week."

"Bitch, if you don't get your ass out this bed, take a fucking bath, and let's go find these damn kids."

Moo was right. I had been in bed, moping around since my kids had mysteriously disappeared, but that wasn't going to do anything for my kids or me. So, today, I would get up and cause hell in the streets of Atlanta.

"Tell Cush to come see me," I instructed Moo.

While she went to get him, I quickly hopped my ass in the shower. I was starting to smell myself, and that was one thing I didn't play about. Stepping into the shower, I let the hot water fall down my body. Rubbing my hands through my hair, I stood there, deep in thought. I didn't think a person would understand the amount of hurt they were causing me. I had been away from my kids the first two years of their life, and I refused to be away from them another day longer.

"What's up, sis?" Cush asked through the bathroom door.

"Let me dry off, and I'm coming out." I stepped out the shower and looked myself over in the mirror. My eyes were puffy and red. I had been crying and sinking into a depression behind this one. It had been some years since I'd felt the amount of hurt I felt right now, and I didn't wish this on my worst enemy.

"What that word is on Joc?"

"He back in Atlanta, but he don't have the twins with him. But, I got something that's going to trip you out."

"What?"

"Lou and Tip out here, too!" I narrowed my eyes at Cush after he said that. The bitch not answering my calls was crazy, but him being in Atlanta was even crazier.

"Find out where he staying and I'ma do a little pop up. What's the word on Dro?"

Of course, y'all know Dro was with Diamond, but he had fucked up and made a baby on her. Times had hit him hard. One, he had to care for a child on his own, which was crazy because the nigga was making enough money to sit down and be a full-time father if he wanted to, but he was greedy and had decided to steal from me as if I wouldn't notice. He fled, and no one had heard from him or seen him since. The history I had with these niggas no longer meant anything. I wanted Joc and Dro dead, and the way Louis was moving, he would be next.

"That nigga vanished off the face of the earth; not even I could find out where he laying low. His mother has his son, and she said he don't call or even stop by to make sure the kid good." Just as I was about to respond, an unknown number called my phone.

"Hello!"

"This Breeze?"

"Yeah, who this?"

"Bitch, stop playing dumb, you know this Kosha."

"Girl, what the fuck you calling my phone for?"

"Tell our baby daddy he got another li'l one on the way."

"Girl, fuck you and Lou! Remember I said your time was limited? Well, time's up, bitch. I'll have your head before the month's out. I am not to be played with."

"You mean, how your trap houses down here being played with? Watch the snakes you keep close to you," she said before hanging up.

"I want that bitch Kosha dead!" I screamed before throwing my phone across the room, shattering it.

"Breeze, I got word that three of your trap houses were robbed and burned down," Moo said with a mug on her face. As many times as I had told her to stay her ass away from the streets, she couldn't let go.

"Bruh, I don't know who the fuck playing with me, but everyone about to fucking die a long, miserable death. Call Louis and Tip. Since they wanna hide out in Atlanta, tell them to get back to White Castle."

"You cut Louis out, Bre."

"Nah, I'll never cut him out, I just be teaching him a lesson. I don't care what the case may be, that nigga has always had my back, and has never let me down. Get him down here now, and tell him it's an emergency. He's not answering my calls."

"Why would I answer your calls and you were in here, fucking the help?" Seeing Louis stand at the door, looking handsome, made me instantly forget he and I were on bad terms. But I was quickly reminded once I saw my twins in his arms.

"Bitch, you took my kids?"

"I didn't think you were worried about them, being that you were fucking on Relle so hard." I was so embarrassed, I chose not to answer him. Moo, Cush, and Tip were all standing in the room, looking at me as if they were shocked. But did they all expect me to just stand around while Louis continued hurting me?

"Don't worry about who I'm fucking on, worry about the fact that

Kosha is pregnant for you, and you aren't even taking care of the two you have."

"Look, Breeze, at this very moment, it's fuck you and Kosha. Give the kids to May, and let's go handle this situation in White Castle. I have run behind you enough, and I have done way more for your bipolar ass than you deserve. No telling how long you and Relle been fucking, and I don't care, I just don't want him around my kids." I didn't even argue with him. I was hurt, but right now wasn't the time to act on emotion, so I simply grabbed my kids out his arms and went downstairs to hand them off to May.

The life I had chosen was a very complicated one, so I had to deal with it. Instead of being a wife, I was a drug lord bitch. I was now the Queen of Cocaine, so whatever came with it, I had to accept it all. I was living in a damn castle with all my family, but that didn't mean a damn thing because the one person I wanted, I had pushed away completely. No matter how many times I said I didn't want him anymore, I always had hopes of us working things out, but this time, we were too far gone. Just like I knew, I think everyone felt the same.

For the first time since I was young, my brother looked at me with so much anger and disappointment in his eyes.

"Come on, the private jet is waiting for us," I said, and everyone grabbed their things and got into their cars.

"I got you, Bre!" Cush knew what to say. Even though I knew he was mad as hell at me, he was always in my corner. I smiled and laid my head down on my brother's shoulder. I could no longer cry over a dead situation. However, I knew this time, I had hurt him, and I was hurting for that reason alone.

SIXTEEN
LOUIS

The plane ride to White Castle was a quiet one, and everyone sat there in their thoughts. It didn't matter how many times I said fuck Breeze, I didn't feel that way, but this time, I was hurt. After everything I had done for her, she had finally gotten me back, and it cut me deep. I wouldn't be able to move past this, but I had no other choice but to try.

I was going to continue to keep the kids, but after Tip had gotten a call about the traps being burned down, I knew sooner or later, she would be calling me. I didn't expect to walk in and hear her speak so highly of me, but not even that made me feel better about what I had seen.

"When the last time you talked to your homie Dro?" Cush asked. I didn't like that nigga because he couldn't stay out of my and Breeze's business, but I guess I had to respect him because he was all she had left.

"I don't know. I tried calling a few times, but I never got an answer. You think he had something to do with this?"

"For his sake, I pray he didn't!"

Dro had long ago disappeared after some money had come up missing. Breeze knew for a fact he had taken it, but I figured he had more money than he could count, so he had no reason to take the money. But, the way he had been moving, I chose not to put anything past him. The nigga had said fuck his kid and was nowhere to be found. He and Joc were missing, but they would soon show their faces around here, and I was sure about that.

Stepping off the plane in White Castle made me realize Atlanta was about to be my new home. I needed to be closer to my kids, and I had to look out for my baby mama. She was making some dumb-ass decisions based off of feelings.

"I'm ready to knock a muthafucka head off!"

"Me too. Shoot the whole fucking block up," Moo said, and Tip looked at her like he had found the woman of his dreams. They would be a force to be reckoned with, and I was going to make sure I stayed out of their way. Moo was a hard head and a hard hitter, and Tip was that times ten.

"Who is that?"

"Breeze's cousin, Big Moo."

"I want her!" I laughed at my youngin, and we kept it pushing. He wanted her, and he would soon get her, but right now was not the time to focus on that. Sooner than later, this would all be over, and everyone could be with who they wanted.

As we approached the car where Relle stood, I noticed the way he looked at me, and I knew I would have to kill him. Breeze was so into her feelings, she couldn't tell this nigga was a snake, but I'd been out here far longer than she had to know the difference.

"You look nice, Boss!" I looked over at Breeze, who was wearing a two-piece Nike outfit with Air Max, and I had to give her props, she did look nice, but Big Buddy was just trying to get under my skin. If Breeze was comfortable with fucking the help, then I'd let it be.

"Thank you, Relle," she smirked.

"What's word on the traps?" Cush asked from behind me.

"Well, right now, I don't have any insight on what's going on. No one is to be found, and everyone I asked, claimed they hadn't seen anything."

"Exactly who did you ask, and where is everyone I had stationed there? I'm confused as to how nobody saw a damn thing." I had to calm Tip down because I could tell Relle had pissed him off, but I wondered the same damn thing. How was it that nobody had seen anything?

"Look, somebody is playing with me, and I know somebody knows something. All of those houses look like a home somebody's grandmother stays in. It doesn't even look like a trap house, so if it was hit, that means the hit came from within the circle. When I found out who it is that's playing this damn game with me, I'm killing them, and if I can't get to them, I'll kill they fucking mama. Playtime is over!" Breeze said as I sat in the backseat of the car and looked at her in awe.

"Take me to Dro's mama house!"

"You sure about that, Boss? That lady is innocent."

The way Relle looked back made me think he had a fucking hidden agenda, and the way Cush, Tip, and Moo looked from me to each other let me know they felt the same. Breeze was mean, but she most definitely wasn't cut out for this job because she couldn't see a snake if it bit her. Unfortunately, she was fucking one. I didn't know if feelings had developed and they were blinding her good judgment or what, but she needed to get it together, and she needed to get it together quickly.

"You heard what the fuck she said, now take her over there before we assume you had something to do with it and blow ya fucking head off." I had heard all about Cush, and we had our disagreements, but I was all for seeing him off this big bear looking muthafucka.

Pulling up to Dro's mama's house took me back to our childhood when we used to sit on the steps and shoot dice with the local homies. I had hoped Dro wasn't playing the games he was playing, but I knew deep in my heart, he was.

We all got out the car, leaving Relle behind, and made our way into the house. Walking in, it was pitch black, but we saw someone sitting off in the corner.

"I knew y'all was coming."

I hit the lights, and the blood that was all over the room was disturbing. I had seen a lot of blood in my time, but it was even worse because it was the blood of his mother and son.

"Bruh, what the fuck has gotten into you?"

"What do you mean, big brother? You chose the side of a bitch that didn't even want to put you on or talk to you for that matter. Had it not been for her coming back to town, me and my girl would still be married."

"What the fuck does that have to do with me? You broke her fucking heart when you decided to have another child on her. That's your problem, not mine, but I'm happy my friend decided to leave your ass, and she found her a real nigga."

"Like who? Diamond ain't shit, and ain't no nigga in their right mind going to put up with all that nagging-ass bullshit she be on."

"Like me, nigga, and a real man don't mind putting up with the nagging," Cush said right before punching Dro in his shit, knocking him out.

"Tie him up, Tip, and bring him in the car. This nigga ain't smart enough to work by himself."

Imagine my surprise when we walked outside, and Relle's ass had left us there. I knew this nigga was on some snake shit, and now I was starting to think he was working with Dro's ass. Maybe that was why he didn't want us to pull up to Dro's mama's house and call his ass out. He was scared of being exposed as well.

Fuck it, I thought.

I went back into the house, in search of Dro's keys. Going into the garage, I jumped into his truck. We would all be jammed packed in that bitch, but it wouldn't be the first time a muthafucka had to sit on somebody's lap to make room.

I would deal with Relle later. White Castle was small, and I knew his big ass wouldn't get far, especially not in a vehicle that was registered to Breeze. These niggas were dumb, and that was why it was so easy to catch on to their little game.

"I can't believe this nigga killed his mother and child," Moo said as she shook her head in disgust.

"You can be with a muthafucka your whole life and not know what they are capable of," I honestly spoke. Dro and I had been friends since we were kids, and just like me, he had a temper, but I never thought he would kill his mother. I didn't know what had gotten into him, but when he woke up, I was going to find out.

Relle

"SO, YOU JUST LEFT THEM THERE?"

"I told you he was too weak for the job, baby."

Joc and this bitch Kosha were getting on my damn nerves. I was never supposed to betray Breeze, but I'd wanted her since her dad had assigned me to be her driver, and not one time did she notice me or look my way.

Joc came to me, getting into my head, telling me how Breeze would pass everything down to Lou, then Lou would cut me loose. I knew that was far from the truth, but at that time, I was weak and wanted nothing more than to remain close to Breeze.

The night we made love, I knew it was only because she was hurt and was all out of options, but I enjoyed it, and I knew she enjoyed it as well.

I tried to get out the deal, but I was in too deep. After the twins went missing, I convinced Breeze that I would go back to White Castle and look for the kids, but the whole time, I was helping Joc and Dro empty out the trap houses. See, Dro knew a little something, but I knew the ins and outs of Breeze's whole operation.

"You was supposed to stay on their asses until we got the fuck away."

"How was I going to stay on their asses and they went in Dro's mama house? It's no escaping them now, we are in too deep. You have no idea what Breeze's li'l short ass is capable of."

"You sound like a pussy. I told Joc you were too soft."

"Did you tell Joc you called Breeze and basically told her to watch her circle?"

"Shut the fuck up, I did no such thing!" she screamed right before she stormed out of the room.

"Breeze ain't shit."

"Neither is a woman scorned, and Kosha is going to be the reason this little plan you have falls through. You sent her to keep Louis busy, but the bitch fell in love. I want out because this is not going to turn out good," I honestly stated.

"Out? My nigga, the only way you can get out of this is if you die, and I'm more than sure you don't want that."

"At this point, I don't care. I've come close to death more times than I can remember. I have traveled all over the world, and have worked close to the King and Princess of Cocaine. That bullet you send my way won't even matter once Breeze and Louis catch up to the both of you."

See, I had prepared myself for this because I knew I would die either way, so him putting a bullet in me wouldn't make his problems go away. I was thirty and had lived a damn good life. I had fucked bitches in different areas and had just recently fucked the baddest bitch on the planet. I was fine with accepting my fate because once Breeze caught on to what we were doing, we would die anyway.

"Nah, I won't kill you just yet. I need you to take me to Breeze."

"I'm not doing it, and sometimes, it's best to just leave well enough alone."

POW!

There was so much more I wanted to say, but I grabbed my chest and looked up at Joc, who stood in front of me with a sinister grin. The bullet had come from behind, but it pierced my soul, and there was nothing more for me to do. I had learned that a consequence always followed betrayal, so I wasn't mad at all. I had been around Breeze long enough to know that everyone's day would soon come, and with Cush by her side, death would soon stare Joc in the face.

I wish I could apologize to Breeze for betraying her, I thought as everything went black, and things around me began to get hot.

SEVENTEEN
BREEZE

"OK, you been sleep long enough. Wake up, bitch," I said, hitting Dro with the butt of the gun, watching him stir out of his sleep.

I waited a while as he focused on everyone around him before he burst out in laughter.

"Breeze, you just know you bad, huh? But this is a man's game, sweetheart."

"Baby, I don't want to hear that, I just want to know where the fuck my money and my drugs are, and who the fuck put you up to playing with me."

"Baby girl, you played yourself when you thought you could run a drug empire by yourself. You a selfish-ass bitch and deserve everything that's coming to you."

POW!

"Oouuuu!" Dro screamed out in pain from the bullet Lou had sent to his right knee.

"Look, brother, we are going to try and make this as easy as possible for you. Breeze has a whole army behind her, so tell her everything she wants to know. We are all tired, and would like to get some rest."

"My nigga, I have nothing to say. She can kill me and I would be just fine. I have nothing more to live for. It was because of that bitch, a nigga went into my mother's home and killed her and my seed. Oh, you thought I did that?"

"Nigga, what the fuck are you talking about?"

"Look, just kill me. Y'all at my neck, but you do know, I didn't know everything about your operation. Remember, you didn't trust the two niggas that had always had your back to know the ins and outs. While you were out here fucking the help, the help was setting you up."

Believe it or not, I'd had a feeling Relle was playing both sides. I saw right through him, and lately, his smile no longer matched his touch. Whenever he ran his hand over my back, it gave me an uncomfortable chill down my spine. My daddy had warned me plenty of times to watch Relle, but I didn't feel the need to since he was the one who had sent Relle to protect me.

"Where the fuck is my money, though?"

"I didn't touch your fucking money!"

"Where the fuck have you been then?" Cush asked as he lit a blunt and passed it to Lou.

"I been out of town. After everything went down, I ran into a drug and gambling problem. I came back into town, looking for Lou at the trap house on Evangeline, only to find out he had taken a vacation. While I was there, it was being raided by Relle and Joc. I know I shouldn't have crossed that line, but I had no money, and I needed a hit. Everyone left and turned their back on me, so since it was fuck me, it was fuck y'all, too."

"Man, I could have gotten you help!"

"You was so caught up in Breeze's ass, you didn't give a fuck. You were the reason I was raising my son solo because you knocked his mama off."

I didn't feel like hearing them have a brotherly debate about betrayal. In my eyes, once you helped the enemy, you were an enemy, so for that alone, I couldn't let Dro live. I emptied the clip into his body and watched as he shook all over the place. Louis would be mad, but I knew he would get over it.

"Clean this up!" I said before stepping over his body. Believe it or not, it was harder for me to kill him than it was for Lou to watch, but he would never understand that the position I had wasn't to be played with. Because I was a female, I had to act first, and never show emotions.

"You didn't have to kill him like that."

"Why you always do that, Lou? Why?"

"Do what?"

"Why the fuck you have to come behind me and question what I do? Everything shouldn't be up for debate. You confused as fuck. Either you gon' ride with me or you gon' be against me. Either way, I'ma still push through this muthafucka."

"I understand what you saying, Breeze, but you heard him. He was forced to do it. He had a problem, and when he needed us, we bust out."

"He had a drug problem and chose to steal. I believe everything he said, but at the end of the day, he didn't have to side with an enemy and bite the hand that fed him."

Now was not the time to get into a debate with Louis about being wrong for killing Dro. The fact of the matter still stood, he was wrong for stealing from me. He knew he would get more had he just asked, but since he and my friend were once married, I would make sure I put him away nicely. He deserved that much, but he didn't deserve to live, and like he said, he no longer had anything to live for.

The ride home was silent, and I couldn't get Relle off my mind. It was like everyone was trying my hand because I was a female, and I was tired of it. The amount of betrayal I'd received would hurt anyone. None hurt more than Lou, though, and even though he had done the same thing over and over again, he was my children's father and my first love. I wanted to stay home and be a mother every day, but instead, I was out here, risking my life. After all this was over, I was done.

I hadn't spoken on it yet, but I was passing my throne to Lou. If needed, I would step up and take a seat beside him, but this was no game for a woman. Ever since it was revealed that this was my empire, I had been tested in more ways than possible.

"You good, sis?" Thankfully, I had kept my house in White Castle, so all of us were there until we came up with a plan to get Relle and Joc.

"Yeah, I just have a lot on my mind."

"Like what? Talk to me. I know I was mad at you earlier when I found out about you and Relle, but honestly, I was mad for that very reason. I knew Bro was a snake, but you couldn't see it, and I waited until he revealed his own hand."

"How is it that everyone knew except me?"

"Because you were blinded by the loyalty you showed them. Everyone not built like you, though, Bre, and people will stay trying you because you a female."

"Yeah, and that's why I'm thinking about stepping down."

"Well, who gon' take over Dad's empire, because the drug game ain't my speed, baby girl."

"Louis." I watched as my brother stared off and stroked his beard as if he were about to protest.

"Baby sis, this ain't even ya big brother speaking, but I'm coming to you as a man. I know how you feel about Louis, and I know how he feels about you, but y'all are too toxic."

"Honestly, this has nothing to do with us. I know for a fact, besides you, Louis has my back, and he won't fuck me over. My heart stopped throbbing for him long ago, but I would be lying if I said he wasn't always one phone call away."

"Well, if you feel he's the man for the job... I know you think things aren't working out in your favor, but you got this, Breeze. You are a beautiful young woman with a handsome son and a gorgeous daughter. I got your back until God call me home, and that won't be any time soon."

"Bro, I'm just ready to give it all up and make sure the kids straight."

"And that's understandable, but be mindful about what you are doing. Daddy worked hard for this, so don't act on your feelings. Think hard before you give everything you worked hard for to a man that you have kids with. I feel Louis is the man for the job as well, but don't act on emotions. An empire can't keep a man, sis." I heard everything Bro was saying, and I would sleep on it, but as of right now, my mind was made up.

Cush

I HAD to make it sound good when Dro was speaking, but no lie, sometimes, I wished I had stayed my ass in Atlanta and never run into Diamond. This relationship thing was new to me, but I believed I was forced into it. Not saying we didn't have good days, because we did, but her nagging was really starting to become a pain in my ass. It was like nothing I did pleased her, and she felt she had to be under me all day.

She had stayed back with May and the twins because she wasn't built for this life, and her judgment of character was bad. She had yet to discover what I did. It was crazy that she thought I was some blue-collar nigga. I had her thinking I was dumb as a box of rocks when it came to this street shit, but the fact of the matter was, I know the ins and outs with my eyes closed.

"What's going on with you and Diamond?" I had been chilling in the room with my sister, running it about her decision to step down. I wasn't against it at all, but Breeze was hardheaded so I would let her make her own decision.

"She cool, but she can get aggravating at times."

"Yeah, but that's Diamond personality. She's harmless and has been through a lot. But if she's doing anything you don't like, you can always tell her."

"Man, that girl crazy. I try to stay clear of her bad side." Just as I was about to finish what I was saying, my phone rang.

"Hello?"

"Well, damn, hey to you, too." Hearing Draya's voice sent me back to a place I didn't want to be. I got up off the bed, covering the speaker of the phone, and went into the other room.

"What's up, Draya?"

"You act like you not happy to hear from me. It's been awhile, baby. I know you not still mad at me."

Hell yeah, I was mad at this bitch. In fact, I was pissed the fuck off at how bad she had played me. Draya was the first woman I'd loved, and she had even given me the idea to give this hitman shit up, but the bitch was grimy and was all about a dollar.

I had gotten into some shit a year ago and had to hide out for a while, but she knew I would be back. The bitch fucked my right-hand man, talking about she wanted to feel the closest thing to me. Bitch sounded stupid as fuck, but Dray wasn't ordinary. The bitch was bad as fuck. She reminded me so much of Dream Doll. I mean, everything about her was on point, but the bitch wasn't loyal, and for that alone, I could no longer fuck with her.

"Hell yeah, I'm still mad at your disloyal ass."

"I told you I'm sorry, baby. How about you come by and see me tonight?"

"See YOUUUUUUUUUU!" I had to hit my Soulja Boy voice on that bitch. She was crazy as fuck if she thought I was about to be in the same room as her and not kill her.

"Man, look, Dray, I'm out of town right now, and I honestly don't think my girl would approve of us meeting up with each other."

"Damn, so it's really fuck me, huh?"

"It's been fuck me since the day you decided to let the homie smash."

"Cush, I'm really going through a lot right now, and I need a friend. We just found out that my dad has stage four cancer, and my mom isn't doing good, either. I need nothing more than support, so if you feel up to it when you get back in town, please pull up on me. You can even bring your girl." Her nutty ass hung up the phone before I could respond. I knew she was trying to trap me, but I didn't think she was that crazy to lie about her parents' health.

"Who was that?" Bre asked when I walked back into the room.

"Draya."

"I know Draya still has a hold on you, and even though she has never done me anything, I will kill her if she thinks she's about to hurt Diamond."

All the women in my life were crazy as fuck, so I wasn't even going to say anything. It was best we focus on the situation at hand, which was finding Relle and Joc. The rest would play out, and hopefully, when it was all said and done, we would be able to live happily ever after.

"Damn!" Breeze said as she jumped from the bed.

"What?"

"I had a tracker placed in Relle's phone and on the car he was driving. I'm about to call Malachi and tell him to track that fat bitch down for me. By tomorrow morning, I'll know where the bitch is located."

"Bruh, and you just remembering that?"

"Yeah, Pops kept telling me to watch out for him, so I decided to track his every move, and my dumb ass forgot."

"A'ight, good job. Well, hit up Malachi, then after that, get some good sleep 'cause tomorrow we will have a long day ahead of us." I kissed her forehead and left the room.

It was crazy how we'd had Relle in the palm of our hands, but somehow, his car had been burned up, and the house his phone was found in was full of blood. Either that nigga was dead, or we were working with a ninja. I could tell Breeze was overwhelmed with everything, but she wouldn't dare speak on it. She didn't have to, though, because even though it wasn't a lot of money and drugs, I would be mad as fuck that somebody had decided to touch what was mine. She just upped the bounty on those niggas' heads, and we all headed back to Atlanta.

I knew I shouldn't have been doing what I was doing, but I had known Draya for a long time and had played a big part in her life. Against my better judgment, I decided to pull up on her and make sure she was straight. I asked the Lord to be with me because I knew I would either kill her for betraying me or dick her down because I couldn't resist her.

"Thank you for coming over!"

"Damn, girl, you could have at least let me knock."

"I heard you when you pulled up."

Draya was one of the baddest bitches on the planet, and I had to give her her props. But, without loyalty, a man would look past all of that ass she carried around with her.

"So, how are your parents doing?" When I turned around, Draya was standing in front of me, ass naked, just like the day she had come into this world. Her pussy was freshly waxed, and her body was glossy like she had taken a shower in baby oil. As badly as I wanted to run out of the door, her dropping to her knees and taking my dick into her mouth immediately stopped me and made me reconsider.

"Shit, girl!" At this point, I wasn't going to stop her. I grabbed her up by her hair and bent her over.

"Slow down, Cush!" I slapped her hand back and drilled the bitch's back in. If she wanted dick that bad, I would give it to her. I could no longer treat Draya like a woman because she had earned the title of a hoe, and that was how I was going to fuck her.

"Damn, daddy, you must miss this pussy."

"SHHHH!" I said as I pulled out and released in her hair.

"Why the fuck would you do that, Cush?"

"Because I treat hoes just like they are. I passed by your parents' house. They looked perfectly fine to me, besides the fact that they said they haven't seen you in a few months. Bitch, all your hoe ass do is lie."

"Cush, I need you, though!"

"Bitch, you had me, but you wanted to fuck behind my back. You down bad, and I can't fuck with you. Now, if you don't mind, my girl is waiting for me to get home."

I left Draya's ass right there on the floor, crying. People always thought about the shit they'd done after the fact. It had been over a year, and Draya had finally decided to reach out and apologize, but before that, she was running around the city with my homie, saying fuck me. I told her karma was a muthafucka.

EIGHTEEN
DIAMOND

Being with a man like Cush was so new to me. He was always so attentive, and I knew sometimes, I could be aggravating, but lately, I had been working hard on trying to change my ways. I was happy that everyone had finally made it back from White Castle, but I was puzzled as to why everyone had come in the house except Cush. I'd really been working hard on not saying anything, but I was pissed the fuck off.

"Where's Cush?" I asked Moo, who was suddenly in love with Tip. I guess a lot had happened when they were away for all those weeks.

"I have no clue." I went to look for Breeze to ask her. I was starting to get pissed the fuck off because I was in the process of trying to change, but if I needed to, I would beat Cush's ass and anybody else in this house if they thought for one second they were about to play with me.

"Breeze, where is Cush?"

"I don't know."

"Everyone in this muthafucka all about a damn game. I bet y'all know where that nigga at and don't want to say anything."

"Calm the fuck down. I got way too much on my mind to even focus on whatever it is you and Cush doing."

"But you covering up for the no-good-ass nigga."

"Covering up? Tf you talking about? If he so damn no-good, why you with him? Girl, you got life and bullshit fucked up. Take your problems up with Cush, not me."

"I should've never dated your brother."

"I was in jail when that decision was made, and I didn't hold a gun to your head. But, you might want to tread lightly if you think that shit gon' fly with him."

I walked out of the room. Everyone in this house was starting to work my fucking nerves. I didn't know why the fuck my hormones had been acting up so badly, but I wasn't about to keep fussing with Breeze about me fucking with her brother. As my friend, if the nigga was a snake, she should have told me what I was getting into.

"Stupid bitch!" I accidentally said aloud as I walked past Moo.

"Who you talking about?"

"No one in particular!"

"Cush got you in here about to get your ass beat, so I'm going to call him and tell him to drop whatever the fuck he doing and come see about you."

"IT'S NOT MUCH he should be doing because, had Breeze not gone to jail, I wouldn't have to deal with this. Cush is not cut out for the streets, and Breeze putting him in this position is dangerous and very selfish on her part."

"Oh, bitch, you're crazier than I thought. Had Breeze not went to jail, you wouldn't even know Cush. And if you think your nigga not cut out for the streets, then it's obvious you don't know your nigga. Matter fact, the shit Breeze do is too slow for him," Moo said with her phone to her ear.

"Cush, come tend to Diamond before I off her. My trigger finger been itching lately," she said, then hung up.

"No need for all that!" I rolled my eyes at Breeze as she walked down the stairs. At that point, I was beyond pissed because it was like everyone knew everything about my man except me, and I didn't like to be kept behind the scenes. I wanted to be on the scenes just like Moo and Breeze were.

"So, Breeze, explain to me what it is that Cush does again."

"That's for Cush to explain. I only came down here because you were speaking very loud."

Look, I wasn't crazy. Being in the midst of Moo and Breeze was something no woman in their right mind wanted. Back in the day, the three of us had stood toe to toe with a lot of niggas and bitches. We had all knocked a few bitches out. I was far from scared, but I knew what the fuck I was up against once they jumped me.

I went into the room and decided to wait for Cush. I was pissed off, and I had many questions for his dumb ass.

When Cush finally decided to come in, it was late as fuck, and as bad as I felt, I wanted to let it go. But had I let him slide with coming in the room smelling just like some cheap-ass perfume, I would forever be mad at myself.

"Was she worth it?"

"Was what worth it? Like, damn, bruh, I just got home, and I'm tired. Let me go to sleep."

I was about to test this nigga's nuts out. I didn't care how many times Dro had disrespected me, no matter what time he came in the house, even he would get in the shower before getting in the bed with me. I needed to know what it was I had done in life to run across so many dog-ass niggas. A bitch from the hood attracted hoe-ass niggas, I guessed.

"Woah, what you doing, Di?"

"Just as I suspected, you a trifling-ass nigga, Cush."

Everything he said as I went into the closet to pack clothes fell on deaf ears. I had done something I promised myself I would never do: I stuck my head under the cover and decided to sniff his dick. The fact that he smelled like perfume and his dick also smelled like pussy with dried-up nut on it let me know he didn't care about my feelings. Him letting me walk out our bedroom and out the house proved that I was once again, in love with a nothing-ass nigga.

I didn't know what I had done to deserve this, but I no longer wanted to be part of this life. After everything Dro had done, I never thought I would be able to love again, then Cush came along and changed my mind. I was loving, sweet, and humble. I gave back to the hood, held my nigga down, and everything else. There was never a time I hadn't come through, so I didn't understand when I had messed up or what I had done to deserve this treatment.

Driving down the street, tears flowing down my face, was blinding me. I promised myself the next relationship I got in, I wouldn't walk out on it. Whatever problems we had, we would talk about it. However, I wasn't about to make the mistake of letting another nigga cheat on me just because I was scared to be single.

I was crying so much, I hadn't even noticed I had run through a red light until it was too late.

BAM!

The crash was a bad one, and as badly as I wanted to get out and run all the way home to Cush, I couldn't. My legs went numb, and my head began to hurt. I had fucked up when I walked out of the house, in my feelings, but at least my pain here on Earth was officially over. If I had time, I would apologize to Moo and Breeze for the words we exchanged, and even hug Cush one last time and do things differently. I would no longer nag him about what he was doing; I would love him like a woman was supposed to love her king.

Lord, forgive me for everything I have done and said, was my last thought before the screams from people went faint in my ears, and everything went blank.

NINETEEN
BREEZE

Getting that call about Diamond had me forgetting she had flashed out at the house. I wasn't mad at her, though. It was no secret that Cush was my brother, and he knew just like I knew I wasn't getting into that shit. At the end of the day, I was a woman, so I understood where she was coming from. She was hurting, and my brother was just dragging her along with the lies he told her. Instead of having her think he was out running the streets with different bitches, he needed to tell her he was a fucking hitman.

"Niggas ain't shit!" Moo said.

"Neither is a woman scorned," I responded as I nodded towards the camera where Draya stood on the other side of my door.

"How the fuck did she know where I laid my head?"

My house was ducked off, and no one outside of the people knew where I laid my head, besides Relle, and that nigga was dead last I heard. I had made sure my shit didn't even come up on the GPS, and I never gave out my address.

"What you doing at my house, Draya?" I said as I swung the door open.

"I heard about your little friend, so I was coming to make sure my nigga was straight. Sorry for your loss, by the way."

"Cush good!"

"Girl, Cush is never good without me, and you know that. He need a real woman on his arms, and nobody in here do shit to make him feel better. Now, if you don't mind, go get your brother and tell him I'm here."

I had no energy to fuss with this nutty-ass bitch, but I wasn't about to allow her in my home, either. I closed the door in her face and went to get Cush. She was disrespectful as fuck, but if I didn't know much about my brother, I knew he didn't play when it came to Diamond. I wanted to see if Draya would still pop that fly shit with Cush like she was popping with me.

"That bitch mad disrespectful, Bre!"

"Yeah, I know, but I just loss my friend, and as bad as I wanted to shoot her, I decided letting Cush handle her would be better."

"Right!"

"I can't go to another funeral, Moo. This shit is getting overwhelming." I laid my head on Moo's shoulder and began to cry. The thing that ate me up the most was the fact that Diamond had left on a bad note with everyone. However, for some reason, I felt like my sister was still alive. We had a connection and a bond, and I had a feeling she needed me, but I wouldn't act on it because I knew it was only wishful thinking.

"Yeah, neither can I, but we will pull through this one like we always do. Did you decide what you were going to do?"

"Yeah, but I won't tell him until after I catch up with Joc's ass."

I had been having a constant battle about stepping down, but in all honesty, I loved this shit, and I was somewhat scared to walk away. I was the Queen of Cocaine, bigger than Griselda Blanco, so you could understand where I was coming from. She pushed weight and had a whole team of men behind her as she did it.

Standing in the position I was in was like being famous, and I didn't want to give my spot up. If I left today and gave all this shit up, would my fans still love me and respect me? Would my men still stand behind me if I needed them? Those were the thoughts running through my mind, but for the sake of my kids and everyone around me, I would let it go. I had conquered a lot, had put a lot of muthafuckas on, caught a few bodies, and had supplied damn near every state in the US, and had even gone to other countries. The only problem everyone had was a girl had a higher seat than most men.

"You don't look like you sure about stepping down."

"Most days, I do have a constant battle with my mind and heart. My heart so fucking deep in this shit, Moo, but I can't attend another funeral. Stepping down is for the safety of you and my kids."

"Don't step down for me because you know I'ma ride this bitch out until the end. Don't step down for your kids because I know you won't let a bitch or nigga touch them. Step down because that's what you want to do. I'm riding with you until the end, and whatever decision you make, I'm standing in your corner. But don't regret handing it all to Lou later. Y'all really need to have a talk because we live in the same damn house, and every day, y'all walk past one another like it's nothing, only talking when it's dealing with the twins."

"We will talk when the time is right, but the man did catch me fucking Relle's ass." We laughed in unison. It wasn't funny at first, but looking back on it now, it was. After all the pussy shit Louis had done to me, I was finally able to see how he really felt about me because he was hurting. But that was the way life worked. I couldn't hold him down all my life when he constantly did the same thing to me.

"Check on Cush and that crazy-ass girl. I don't want to lay hands on her. I'm about to try and take a nap since May got the twins." I hugged Moo and stood to leave. I hardly ever showed my friends affection, but the way Diamond had left us had me wanting to hug them every chance I got. I was mad at myself for getting Diamond caught up in this life, and even though it might sound crazy, I was happy my friend hadn't died from a gunshot because of a pussy nigga trying to get at us. That would have devastated me even more that I had gotten someone so sweet and innocent caught up in our crossfire.

Three months later

"Bitch, this the third damn note I've found today."

"You must have a secret admirer."

Since Diamond's funeral, things had been different for everyone. Cush was still staying in the house, but he hardly ever came out of the room or talked to us. Just as I expected, he had put a toe tag on Draya's ass a few days after the funeral because she had shown up, talking shit.

My brother was in a bad place, and to make things worse, they'd had a closed-casket funeral. The last time I saw my friend's beautiful face was the day she died. The coroner said her body was badly burned, and that nothing was left but ashes.

"What does it say?"

"They all say the same thing," I said to Moo. Lately, I had been receiving notes here and there, but they didn't make any sense, and I was kind of on edge because somebody had been following me and even knew where I laid my head.

"I got something you want!" I read the note off to Moo and threw it out the window. I wasn't in the mood for fucking guessing games. If anyone had anything for me, they would soon show their face, but I was not about to keep looking over my shoulders. I would fuck around and kill anybody who thought they were about to play with me.

Stupid bitches! I thought just as my phone vibrated, alerting me that I had a text.

Louis: Hey, I know things been weighing you down, so would you like to go out for drinks and some food tonight?

I kind of smirked reading Louis' text. We had been getting along well. However, we weren't having sex; everything was strictly about the kids. He had really been by my side since Diamond's death and had even become a brother to Cush. Never thought I would see the day that happened, but I was happy as hell everyone was getting along.

Me: Yes, I need a few shots.

Louis: Cool, be ready for 8!

"Who got you over there blushing all hard?"

"Lou just asked me to dinner, and I wasn't blushing, bitch."

"The hell if you weren't!" I didn't even answer her ass, I just turned the music up, and lit a blunt. I felt really good about this date tonight. Louis had been showing me a different side of him, and I knew it was the babies who had turned him around, but I didn't want to get too deep with him again. There was nothing wrong with us being friends, though.

TWENTY
JOC

Every day, I followed Breeze around, and the bitch seemed like she was unfazed by it. I had hit up at least three of her traps, and the money and drugs I had taken hadn't even broken her down. That was how I knew she was sitting filthy. But I had something she wanted, and it would make her crack.

"Shut the fuck up!" I screamed as I kicked Diamond, who had been crying since the day I pulled her out of her car. You would think she would be used to being with me, but every day, she cried more and more. I even fed her ungrateful ass. I know y'all are wondering whose body was in that car. I got tired of Kosha talking about Louis' ass all day, so I killed the bitch and rode around with her body in the trunk. I was happy as hell that I was following Diamond when she had that wreck.

"Just let me go, Joc. I won't say anything."

"How do Breeze even hang with someone as weak as you? You have no fight in you, baby girl," I said as I looked at her fragile body.

I walked out of the room, locked the door, and went back to doing what I had been doing for the past few months. Following Breeze around was like a full-time fucking job, but the bitch never had her kids, and she hadn't led me to where she kept all her drugs. I needed to come up with a plan to get more money from her. The ransom notes I had been leaving for her weren't making her move like I thought they would.

Driving down Loyal Drive, I wondered if the beef I had caused with Breeze was worth it. I knew once they had caught up with me for the way I had done Diamond, everything would be over, but I had no money to leave, so until they finally accepted my demand, I would stay behind and just wait.

TWENTY-ONE

TIP

I had chosen not to say anything because the death of Diamond was still so fresh, but one night, I had gone outside to look for a cigar in my car and saw a car parked across the street. I didn't speak on it because I didn't think anything of it, but after seeing the bitch again, and then Moo telling me Breeze was receiving random notes, I decided to sit in my car all night and see if I would catch something. Imagine my surprise when I saw Joc's scary ass. However, when I followed him to an abandoned house, I got an even bigger surprise. I jumped out of the car and followed him, but when I peeped through the cracks and saw Diamond on the floor in fetal position, I immediately put my plan into motion.

"What's going on?" I dapped Cush up as he sat across from me. I had been sitting on the house Joc was at all night. I needed to get his routine down packed. I needed to know how he was moving, and from what I saw, it wasn't very smart.

"Big Brother, I know you don't want to hear this, but Diamond not dead." I saw him getting ready to flash out, so I quickly continued because I didn't want to put a bullet in my brother's head today.

"Look, lately, Breeze been getting little petty notes here and there, but she never said anything. Moo told me. The only reason I decided to look into it further is because I caught a car outside the crib a few nights, and only a few people know where we lay our head. I think he holding Diamond on ransom or some shit."

"Man, where this nigga at? I want to get at him right now."

"I know you do, but let's get Diamond and let Breeze handle that nigga. I know she'll get a kick out of torturing his ass."

The only reason I would let Breeze off him was because he had put her through the most pain. He had taken damn near everything that meant something to her, so killing him might lighten her spirit.

"Yeah, let her get her last kill before she steps down."

"What you talking about, Big Brother?"

"Nothing. She will speak to y'all soon, but come on, let's get out of here. I need to get my girl back. A nigga never know how they really feel about someone until they are taken from you and a hole is left where the love once was."

Big brother was speaking some real shit, and to be fair, I felt the same way about Moo. She had come along and made me want to change all my player ways. Plus, the girl was crazy as fuck, and she had some good pussy between her legs. I was wild and had different women, but since getting with her, all that had changed.

"You gon' call Breeze right now, or you want to get in there and get Diamond first?"

"Let's stake that nigga crib out, wait until he come home, then we will go in and grab him and Diamond. Kill two birds with one stone."

I nodded in agreement before taking a shot of Hennessey. We were both already dressed in all-black, so there was no need to go back to the crib. He left his car and hopped into the beat-up Altima I had copped from a little chick who stayed in the projects.

On the way to Joc's crib, I couldn't help but think about what Cush had said about Breeze stepping down. I hoped she chose wisely with whatever decision she made.

"THERE THAT NIGGA GO RIGHT THERE." Cush and I had been sitting outside of Joc's house for hours, waiting for him to get back. We could have easily gone and gotten Diamond, then get Joc another time, but Cush felt if we let him go this time, we might not ever find him again.

"'Bout time. The fuck he been doing?"

"The nigga is crazy, so while we staking his shit out, he was probably watching our shit."

We jumped out and went in behind Joc, kicking the door in. If only y'all could've seen the look on that nigga's face. Niggas acted so hard until their demons caught up with them. He just knew for a fact he was going to get away with everything he had done, but we had only let the bitch get comfortable. Beef was never dead with us; it always just down for a minute.

I kept my gun drawn on him as Cush went from room to room to look for Diamond until he found her. Walking back into the room, I couldn't stand to look at her. Diamond had been beaten and had been left to sit in her own blood. The look on my brother's face let me know he didn't know if he would be able to wait until Breeze made it to kill this bum.

"Come on, buddy, you coming with us, and you better hope my homie don't do you like you did his girl."

"It ain't even gotta be all of this!" I punched him in the back on the head because I couldn't believe this bitch was begging for his life after everything he had done. This nigga had to help me understand how it didn't have to be like this. I wanted to kill him just for saying something so damn stupid. Honestly, I just wanted to kill somebody. I had so much on my mind, and to make matters worse, my mother had been blowing my phone up.

She had been begging me to come meet with her, and I felt it was time. I needed closure, but I also needed to know why my mother would do what she did to me. I was just a child, and she was supposed to protect me. Instead, she had taken my innocence from me.

Choosing not to tell anyone, I decided I would catch a flight later tonight and go meet up with her tomorrow. I didn't want my mother to be a part of my life in any way, shape, or form but there was so much I needed to know. It was the kid in me who was reaching out to her.

Breeze

MY NIGHT with Louis was great, but I was still holding this wall up. I knew it was crazy because I had really seen a change in him, and my heart wanted him. However, my mind was holding me back. I was having a battle between my mind and heart. He was the man I wanted to be with, but I needed reassurance that he would never turn his back on me again.

All that aside, Christmas had come early for me, so when Cush called, I got dressed in my best attire. I put on an all-white, two-piece pants suit, a pair of Red Bottoms, and a big rim hat. I wore my hair in a low ponytail. I left out of the house without telling anyone where I was going. Louis wanted a piece of Joc, too, so I knew he would be mad, but I needed to handle that nigga myself. I needed Joc to feel me and to feel everything he had put me through.

Earlier, we had found out Diamond was pregnant, and because of how he had sexually abused her and beaten her, she had lost the baby. My brother was devastated, but the amount of pain he had brought to Diamond outweighed my brother's feelings.

I walked into the warehouse where he was tied up and stared at him. Cush and Tip had beaten him so badly, it was hard to recognize who he was. I placed my hat on the table and began to kick him until he woke up. It was crazy how after everything Joc had put me through, a part of me couldn't kill him. I faulted myself for the way he was around here acting because I had laughed in his face instead of being his woman and making sure my dad didn't short him.

I stood in front of the devil with my gun drawn, tears running down my face. I just wanted to know why. I needed to know why he had done so much to me. Before all the beef, we were actually in love, or at least I thought we were. But the amount of anger and hurt he showed towards me had me thinking it was all just a game.

"I thought you was a boss," he laughed. "You ain't pull that trigger yet. You couldn't kill me if you wanted to. You were out here trying to play with the big dogs, but have no heart."

"I want to know why, Joc. Explain to me why you would try and hurt me the way you did."

"Bitch, you were hurt? Imagine the amount of hurt I felt when my bitch walked in and cut my supply short. If you gon' kill me, then do that, because I won't give you an apology for anything I did. You are weak, Breeze, and the position you have is not for a woman."

I lowered my gun because he was right. At that very moment, my reason for not killing him wasn't because I was weak or wasn't boss enough, but because I loved him at one time, and considered him a close friend. My heart was bigger than any drug I'd touched.

I fell to my knees and cried, and at that very moment, I knew it was time I talked to Lou.

"See, bitch, I knew you couldn't kill me. You are still the same weak, ugly, dumb bitch—"

POW!

I jumped up at the sound of the gun and looked over at Joc's lifeless body lying there. His last words to me weren't pleasing, but that would be between him and his God.

Scared to see where the bullet had come from, I stood there in a daze.

"I told you I got you. Stop running and let me love you. Let me kill for you. I know I've hurt you, but I'm a changed man, and I'm trying to show you." Louis stood behind me, speaking those words. I had been running from him because I was scared of being hurt again.

I slowly turned around with tears still rolling down my cheeks.

"I'm scared," I said right above a whisper.

"Scared of what? Of me, or being hurt again? You have nothing to be scared of. I know I may have fucked up, but I'm nothing like them other niggas, Bre. We are both grown, and will soon be hitting thirty, so if I'm with you, I'm with you and nobody else. Kids are now involved, and I want my family. I want you to be my wife. Stop running and let me in."

I just stood there, not saying anything. I wanted to, but I choked on my words and couldn't at the moment. Instead of responding, I walked past him. With one hand on the door, my back still to him, I said one last thing before walking out.

"Call the cleanup crew." Louis was still my worker and would act as such. I placed my hat on my head, and glasses on my face. My heart was black and cold. I no longer felt the love anymore. It was crazy, though, because I had so much love for Louis, I was just scared of being hurt again.

The ride home was a quiet one, and I wanted to be in my thoughts. It was crazy how I had walked away from this man, but would literally have a heart attack if he were to get with someone else. I really needed to get my shit together and go get my damn man. Hell, I might as well give him another try. One thing about it, if my heart didn't jump for him, my pussy sure wanted that big muthafucka he walked around with between his legs.

I was in my thoughts about Joc being gone, and I couldn't believe this was what it had come to. Money and power brought out the worse in people, and he was one who didn't respect the fact that I held the position I had. Funny how you could be with somebody and never know how they feel about you. My gut told me that even though Joc was dead, this thing was far from over. I had to secure my business, and everything around me, so it was time for me to finally stop going back and forth in my mind and step down.

Me: Hey, we need to talk.

I sent Louis a text and waited for him to reply. There was so much for us to talk about, and hopefully, he would forgive me for the way I had been acting. It was now time for me to face my demons and believe that maybe he could change. Once he didn't reply to my text, I knew he was mad, but I wouldn't deal with that today.

TWENTY-TWO

TIP

I didn't want to meet up with my mom because the bitch was crazy, and I wasn't in the mood to hear what she had to say. How could I face my mother after everything she had put me through?

I sat at Pluckers and waited until my mother came. I refused to meet with her in private. I didn't trust her, and for all I knew, the bitch was trying to fuck with me again.

"Hey, son," she said as she tried to give me a hug. I dodged her because I wasn't in a place where I forgave her just yet.

"Too soon for that. I just want to know why you wanted to see me."

"It's been a long time since we've talked. You left that day and never came back, and now I hear you been running with Breeze and her brother, Cush."

"What that have to do with you?"

"What do you know about them?"

"So you called me here to ask about them? How do you even know Cush? He's not from down here."

"Actually, I called you down here because, like I asked, what do you know about them?"

"Nothing much, but Breeze looked out for me, and so did Cush."

"Well, I never thought I would have to have this conversation with you, and I'm not sure if they know or not, because Lorez was a lying-ass nigga. Back in the day, Lorez and I used to fuck around, and I ended up pregnant with you. Once I called and told him about being pregnant, he skipped states, and I haven't heard from him since. He did the same to Breeze. Poor child damn near raised herself. It wasn't until she was older that he decided to be a part of her life."

I took in everything my mother said and, to be honest, I wasn't shocked at all. There were a few people who had said Cush and I resembled each other. She could have told me this over the phone because sitting across the table from her wasn't very pleasing.

"Yeah, but that didn't give you a reason to do what you did."

"Son, I was sick, and you have to forgive me. The day you left, I checked myself into rehab and been on my medicine since then."

None of that gave a mother an excuse to do what she had done to her son. I would holla at Breeze and Cush when I got back home, but I could no longer sit across from her. My mother was no longer my mother, but a stranger off the street. I threw some money on the table and got up without so much as a goodbye, and went to catch my flight back to Atlanta.

Back in Atlanta

"Bae, you good? You been quiet since you got back home."

Moo was a different breed. She was hood as fuck, but the prettiest woman I had ever seen. She was short, with caramel, blemish-free skin, hair down her back, a plump ass, and plump lips to match. Meeting her was a relief from life because before she had come along, I was running with a different woman every day, not thinking I would ever settle down.

"Yeah, I'm good. I went and hollered at my mom today."

"Oh, well, when will I get to meet her?"

Moo or no one else knew the hell my mama had put me through, and I didn't want to say anything. I was afraid of being judged or looked at as if I were stupid, but everyone in this bitch had problems they were dealing with. This was one dysfunctional-ass family, but I was happy as hell to be a part of it.

"Breeze and Cush here?" I ignored her question. I would tell her soon, but right now was not the time. Once I spoke with my sister and brother, I would run everything down to her.

"Yeah, they both in the basement."

See, what people didn't know was Breeze kept her supply in the basement of the house, and we had to go through her master bedroom closet to get to it. She was smart when it came to business, and for that, I respected her on a different level. She was always two steps ahead of the game, and she kept her moves to herself.

"I'm going to holla at them, then I'll be back up to holla at you," I said and smacked her on the ass before I got up to leave.

"I'm happy it's just the two of y'all down here because I wanted to holla at y'all about something."

"What's up, young blood?" Cush always called me that like he was so much older than I was.

"I went to meet my moms, and she ran some shit down to me. She basically said that the two of you are my siblings." They didn't look shocked, so I knew then they knew but hadn't said shit to me.

"Dad told me to get you off the corner when he saw you. He ran everything down to me, so I got you and put you on. I made sure you were straight and made sure Lou looked after you while I was locked up. I wanted to tell you, but I was waiting until the right time."

"So why didn't he tell me?"

"That was Lorez's way of moving. He didn't mean any harm by anything he did. He did the same to me, but had he not stepped in when he did, I probably would have taken my own life or drank myself in a coma. Cush, on the other hand, had been around, but he, too, made sure you were good."

"I understand that, but when were y'all going to tell me?"

"Once all this shit was over."

"It's over, and y'all still ain't say shit. Do y'all know the craziness I had to go through coming up?"

"Calm down, li'l brother."

"Don't 'li'l brother' me, Cush. I had a rough-ass childhood. My fucking mother raped me every damn day until I was old enough to run away. I appreciate you for saving me, but would you have done that if Lorez didn't tell you to?"

"I would have taken you off the corner, no doubt, because you still a young bull. But no, I wouldn't have promoted you off the block."

"DAMN! Like that, huh?"

"It's no way, Tip, it's business. You a bull, my nigga, I give you that, but I got niggas that's been around longer than you have so I could have chosen anybody. I'm sorry you had to go through everything you went through, but we all had a fucked-up childhood. I didn't have a mom at all."

I heard everything Breeze was saying, but I needed time for everything to register. The happiness I felt right now was the best feeling ever, but a part of me wished they had said something.

"Look, I know this will take a lot of time to register, but just know we always got your back, and Lorez had your back as well. Don't feel like you don't mean shit to us because you our li'l brother, and we love you."

"Oh, and how do you want your mother handled?" I didn't know if I wanted to tell Breeze to let her ride or kill her, but I knew a person like my mother couldn't walk these streets. If she had done it to her son, there were many other little boys she would do it to.

"You can do whatever you want."

"Bet! Cush, handle that once we finish down here." It was like a weight had been lifted off my shoulders at that very moment, and for the first time, I felt like a new person.

"So, Breeze, what you gon' do? You gon' stay in, or you getting out?"

"Nah, baby bro, this is not my lane anymore, and y'all have too many problems. I feel like y'all mama instead of a damn queenpin."

"Well, you are a mother now."

"Shut up, Cush! Tip, place those bricks in them bags for me and get them to the Jamaicans." Just like that, it was back to business with Breeze, and that was how it had always been.

Diamond

SOME DAYS, I woke up in a cold sweat, thinking Joc would someday come back and get me. I knew Breeze had told me over and over again he was dead and wouldn't come back, but those days were pure hell for me. For the longest, I was mad at everyone because I thought they didn't care about me being out there, all alone, until they showed me my obituary.

Cush said he wasn't mad, but he hadn't slept in the same bed as me since I'd come home, and I heard him crying about the baby I had loss one night. To make matters worse, the doctor said, with the amount of damage Joc had caused, I might not be able to carry again. At that point, I was no longer a real woman, and I knew Cush would hate me. I wanted to think differently, but after all I had been through, he was turning his back on me.

"How you holding up?" Moo and Breeze came in every day. Moo more than Breeze, but after all, I had to understand she was a businesswoman. I didn't want to seem selfish, but it was like the people I needed the most were no longer there. I needed their moral support right now, and they were too blinded by everything else.

"You know I have my days," I shrugged.

I didn't really feel like talking, so instead, I turned over on my side and turned off the lamp that sat on the nightstand. I had no intentions of being mean to Moo or anyone because I knew them not being around was them giving me space. But after losing a baby, and being raped every damn day, I felt so alone sometimes.

"Diamond... Diamond, you good?" I jumped out of my sleep to see Cush and everyone else standing over me.

"Yeah, what's going on?" I sat up in bed, and it was wet. This was nothing new, but most nights, I was able to have the sheets and mattress washed before sunlight rolled in.

"Diamond, you were literally screaming in your sleep." For the first time, I noticed the worry in Breeze's eyes, but I just wanted them to get out before they noticed I had pissed in the bed.

"I'll be good. I was probably just having a nightmare. Thanks for all your concern, but I really want to go back to bed."

"You sure, Di? I can sleep with you tonight."

"Yeah, Bre. Thank you, though." I wanted to reach out to my best friend so badly and tell her I needed her shoulder right now, but I chose to let it go and talk to her later. Cush hadn't even stayed behind to make sure I went back to sleep. He left the room before everyone else, not even looking behind to see if I was okay. But, I couldn't trip on him. He was a man before anything, and I knew he would one day want a child, but I had been robbed of that.

Once everyone was gone, I jumped out of the bed to lock the door, then I went into the bathroom to take a shower. I needed to get everything cleaned before someone noticed what was going on.

Getting out the shower, I looked at the clock on the nightstand and noticed it was going on three in the morning. I had more than enough time, so I moved quickly.

Walking out of the room, I could have burst into tears when I saw Cush sneaking a woman out of the house. Instead, I locked eyes with them, giving off a smirk, and went to wash my sheets.

"I can't believe this keeps happening to me," I said to myself loudly.

"When were you going to tell me you were still having nightmares?" I shrugged and went into my room to place some new sheets on the bed. Now I was kind of happy I hadn't opened up to anyone. Maybe he felt that since I damn near never came out of the room, I wouldn't see anything, but what was done in the dark always comes to light.

"You don't hear me talking to you, Di?" Cush said as he grabbed me by the arm.

I reached over and grabbed the fingernail file and cut him with it. "As long as you live, don't you ever put your fucking hands on me again. I will kill your disrespectful ass and smile in my mugshot."

"You bugging, ma. It don't even have to be all of this." The look Cush wore on his face let me know he was hurt, but his pain didn't measure up to the amount of betrayal I felt right now, so he could miss me with the puppy dogs eyes.

"You might want to go get that checked out and get the fuck out my face."

"You right, ma. I'ma fall back. I don't have time for your games anymore, anyways. I need a grown woman, not some little-ass girl that shut off the world when things aren't going her way. When you grow the fuck up, then you can holla at me." He didn't even give me a chance to respond. How was I running away from things when he hadn't even been by my side since finding out I had loss the baby? It wasn't my damn fault. I needed him more than ever. He didn't see that, though, because he was so busy making sure his bitches were good.

Fuck them and this damn house.

I grabbed a bag and packed a few outfits. I knew I shouldn't leave because the last time I left, I had damn near died, but I couldn't be around so many selfish muthafuckas anymore.

I HAD BEEN LAID up in the hotel for a damn week. I had turned my phone off because I was tired of Cush texting me, calling me every name in the book besides a child of God. I didn't have time for him because if he cared that much, he would have made sure I was straight, but he hadn't. Instead, he was checking for other bitches. Cush could kiss every part of my ass. If that was what he wanted, then he was a free man.

Life was so lonely for me, and had I known it would be this way, maybe I would have forgiven Dro and accepted the baby. That was neither here nor there because they were both gone.

Laying in this bed with my phone off and without a million people around me gave me time to think about everything. I would be lying if I said I wasn't hurting because I was. In fact, I was hurting and alone in this world, but nobody knew that because everyone had their own damn problems.

Today, I had finally decided to go back to the house. I'd had enough space to know exactly what I wanted. I was no longer going to stand for letting a man disrespect me. If I was dealing with karma, then I would do so peacefully because being with a man wouldn't make or break me.

"Where the fuck you been, Diamond? Everyone been worried sick about you," Breeze said as soon as I walked through the door.

"Everyone like who? Like you, or like Cush, because y'all didn't even notice I was here."

"Diamond, you my friend, but bitch, I'm real tired of you popping off at the mouth when you have a problem with Cush. Whatever the two of y'all got going on is strictly between y'all. I have enough problems of my own."

"Nah, sis, let her finish saying how she really feel. We all know every time Diamond get mad, her true feelings about you come out. She don't really fuck with you, sis; you been helping dead weight all this time."

"That's enough, Cush. I don't need the home team beefing." Breeze walked off, but not before looking at me with a mug. I knew what Cush had said made her feel some type of way. "Oh, and Diamond, you got one more time to disrespect me, and I will forget we were ever friends."

Truthfully, I wasn't even mad at Breeze, but more so myself. I was pissed at myself for getting my feelings involved with another bitch-ass nigga. My only fuck up was he and my best friend were brother and sister.

"You know, Diamond, I understand you went through something, but the way you walking around here acting is real fucked up," Cush had the nerve to fucking say.

"The way I've been acting? Bitch, I sat there and watched you walk a girl out the house while I was washing pissy sheets. In case you didn't know, I have been pissing on myself since that stupid-ass accident."

"Don't you think I'm hurting behind what happened to you, too? I don't even know what to say to you because you are not the only one that took a loss."

"You didn't have to say shit to me but be there. I just needed you, but instead, you wanted someone else. All I've ever wanted was for a man to have my back and protect me." I was crying so hard, but when Cush came to hug me, I fought him off. Cush didn't know how much I needed him. I had never been through so much horror in my life. Every damn day, I fought for my fucking life, so the moment I got out, all I wanted was my man.

"Look, Cush, you just put up with the loss of our baby, but I don't think you understand what I went through in that house. I love you, but you got to understand me when I tell you that I don't trust you anymore. To protect my sanity and my peace, I'm choosing to walk away from this."

"How you just gon' decide to do what's best for you, as if I don't have any feelings?"

"Baby, you been said fuck me. You said fuck me the day you walked a female out this house and looked at me as if I was just a guest in your home." There was nothing else for us to talk about, so I walked away.

Cush had the nerve to act like he was the fucking victim when I had been the one hurting. That stupid-ass bitch had let me suffer while he was out having the time of his life, so now it was my turn to watch him suffer. Call me crazy, but I wasn't ready to give up on him. He would suffer by watching me transform into the old Diamond, however.

I would soon apologize to Breeze, but right now, I needed to get my mind together. She knew I didn't mean any harm by anything I had said, but on a serious tip, I felt nobody was in my corner. Maybe I was in my feelings, I don't know, but I would talk to her about everything that had been going on later.

"You rolling with us to the party tonight?" Moo asked with a slight attitude.

"Yeah, what time we leaving?"

"Around nine. And, look, I understand you been going through some things, but try to let it all go and just enjoy yourself because lately, your attitude has really been fucked up."

"Yeah, I know."

It was already after five, so once Moo left the room, I went to find something to wear. I had chosen black Adidas pants, a pair of black pointed-toe Red Bottoms, and a white muscle shirt that was cut to reveal my stomach.

Tonight would be a good night, and I knew Cush would be in the building, but he would regret fucking me over this time around.

"THIS BITCH LIT!" I screamed over the music.

I didn't even walk to the VIP section with the other girls. This was my first time out in forever, so I was about to fuck the dance floor up. I had two shots of Patrón in my hands, and a few fine-ass niggas crowded around me. Cush who? I was fucking shit up and felt like, fuck everything a bitch nigga had put me through.

"Cush flashing out, Di, you might want to calm down," Breeze said as she approached me. See, this was what I meant. I knew Cush was her brother, but damn, I was her best friend, and she should stay out of our mix.

"Lord, I came here to have a good time. I'm not focused on Cush or what he has going on. Now, if you don't mind, let me enjoy myself."

"Girl, you really full of your-fucking-self. You popping slick and just don't know that nigga you fucking with has an aim like no other. Cush is a fucking paid hitman and has killed bitches for little to nothing, so please don't think he won't knock you off for playing him." She was in my face as if she were about to hit me, but the way I felt, I would fuck Breeze's ass up.

"Like I said, I'm not worried about Cush."

I turned back around and began to dance with some random-ass man. Just a few nights ago, he was sneaking a bitch out of the house, and now he wanted to be in his feelings about me dancing and enjoying myself. Well, he might as well sit back and enjoy the show because I was about to give his ass something to look at.

My eyes were closed, and I was having a blast, but I smelled Cush before I saw him. By the time I opened my eyes, he was knocking the dude out I had been dancing with and had grabbed me by my arm. I fought Cush's ass all the way out of the club, but his strength overpowered me.

Back in the days, I had gotten down with both men and women, but this nigga was nothing to play with, and when I looked up at him, his light-brown eyes were now black and held no emotion.

"Get the fuck in the car." I had never seen this side of Cush, and I remembered what Breeze had said. Instead of putting up a fight, I got into the passenger side of his Challenger and braced myself for what would come next.

"Cush, slow down!" He was flying, swerving in and out of traffic without blinking. This nigga was really crazy, and right now, I was scared for my life. I had just beaten death, but at this very moment, I felt like I was sitting next to the Grim Reaper, and I couldn't escape whatever he had in store for me.

Cush

"FUCK, FUCK, FUCK." I beat the steering wheel over and over as I sat outside the house. There was no doubt in my mind I was going to kill Diamond for playing with me, but I loved the dumb bitch too much to knock her off. She had better been lucky, too, because I'd killed bitches I'd known longer than her and thought nothing of it.

"Do you think I'm some mark-ass nigga, Diamond?" For the first time since I'd dragged her out the club, I looked her way and noticed how scared she was.

"Answer me! You was big bad when Breeze came down there, so talk now."

"Does it really matter at this point, Cush? I said you and I were over, so it really doesn't matter what I think of you. Did you think I was some weak-ass bitch?"

"I think nothing less of you, you think low of yourself. You put yourself down. We were both hurting, but you getting beside yourself and about to end up with nothing. The only reason I came and snatched your ass up was because I wanted to talk to you about the way you been acting. I heard you loud and clear when you said we were over, and I respect that, but as a woman, you shouldn't be in the club, wilding out the way you were."

I had to stop talking and take a damn breather. Diamond had me so damn pissed off, I was literally on ten. But, I knew I needed to talk to her because she was about to fuck around and be in this world by her-damn-self. She had been popping stupid with both Breeze and Moo, and the only thing saving her was years of friendship.

"Look, I know you hurt about everything that happened to you, but if you would stop acting off emotions, that wouldn't have happened. You being mad at me is perfectly fine, because I know I deserve it, but the way you treating Breeze and Moo is a different story. You need to fix that and stop blaming my sister for what is going on between us. At the end of the day, you have to respect the fact that she's my sister. But believe it or not, she's always on my ass about treating you right."

"Cush, it was never supposed to be like this. I was so hurt from my last relationship, I wanted everything we had to be perfect."

"It could have been, Diamond, but your insecurities wouldn't allow it. I'm sorry you had to see what you saw, but honestly, every time I tried to be there for you, you pushed me away. We were both hurting. I loss a child the same day you did, so why was it you were the only one who was able to mourn that loss?"

"I just felt like you didn't care, Cush. It was so many nights I cried out for you. It was hell in that house with Joc. I wanted you, and I needed you. The day you came and got me should have been the best day of my life, but it wasn't, because it was too late. I knew I had loss the baby. I laid on the floor, balled up in a knot as the blood rolled down my legs. I cried out for you, Cush. I needed you. I wanted you."

It was crazy how one minute, I wanted to knock her head off her shoulders, and the next, I was sitting in the car, crying with her. This was the first time I had cried since I'd found my mother dead when I was just a kid. To lose a child was another level of pain, though, and this was something I didn't wish on anyone. I knew it was time for me to be a man instead of acting like a damn boy, though.

"Diamond, I know I been a fuck up lately, and for that, I'm sorry, but I need you to know I love you with everything in me. The loss of our child fucked me up, too, I just didn't know how to cope with the pain of losing something so precious. We all thought you were dead; they even said your body had burned to ashes. I was weak without you, so never for a moment think I was over here, happy and living life while you were suffering," I truthfully spoke. Diamond brought out the real in me, and when she was gone, I felt like I had nothing more to live for. I was picking up hit after hit just to keep my mind off everything going on around me.

"I just want you to promise me you will always love me."

"I got you, Di. I love you with every part of me, and I promise to never hurt you again." I leaned over and kissed her soft, plump lips. It had been so long since I'd felt Diamond, and I couldn't wait to get her in the house and break her hard-acting ass down. She missed Daddy's dick, but I was going to give it to her so she could start acting right.

"You need to talk to Breeze, too, because right now, she not fucking with you at all. You know how she is when she says she's done with somebody. The only muthafucka that can slide with playing with her is Lou because everyone else is a no-go."

"Damn, she that mad?"

"Yeah, you been in her house, disrespecting her. I would be mad, too. But that club situation is what really drew the line for her. Now, come on so I can beat that pussy up."

I was sure she and Breeze would talk one day, but Diamond, out of all people, knew how Breeze got down. Loyalty and respect were everything to her, so once she felt you'd crossed her in any way, she was done with you.

In the club, I'd had to literally beg Breeze not to shoot Diamond or put her out of the house. That was the only reason I had grabbed her out of the club. Di was bugging hard, but Breeze wasn't feeling her, and she knew all she had to do was say the word, and one of her niggas would kill Diamond in the blink of an eye. Bre was sweet and loyal as fuck, but if you got on her bad side, you would think you were playing chess with the devil. She was worse than I ever was.

Breeze

I DIDN'T KNOW what the fuck Diamond was on, but I was going to fuck around and put her in her place. I had gone back and told Cush what she'd said, and he decided to handle it because I was going to literally kill the bitch if she jumped stupid with me one more time. I was more laid back; I wasn't the friend who was always in your business. Diamond knew Cush was my brother when she got with him, so I didn't understand why she blamed me for everything he had done to her. The most I could do was tell him when he was wrong, but at the end of the day, he was a grown-ass man, and I had problems of my own.

I had been going back and forth with Louis' dumb ass for years so I would be a different type of stupid if I told her to leave Cush. How the fuck could I tell somebody to leave their nigga when I was still trying to get mine to act right? So, I stayed out of their business for that reason.

"What you gon' do about Diamond?" Moo asked.

"Nothing, I just need time away from her. The house is big enough for me not to see her." I had my own wing in the house, and the only way I would see any of them was if I went downstairs to the kitchen or left out the door. My kids and Louis had rooms on my wing, and I made sure not to see him as much, so you know I was going to put extra effort into not seeing Diamond.

"I think you should just put her out."

"Nah, she only has us so I won't do her like that, but I'm not fucking with her at all right now."

When I walked into the house, I rolled my eyes and kept walking. I had just said I was trying to avoid Diamond, but she and Cush were sitting in the living room as if they had been waiting for me to walk through the door.

"Told you to just put her out," Moo whispered from behind me.

I wouldn't have to put her out because I was about to walk straight past her as if I didn't see her. It was going on four in the morning, and I was tired, so she would have to wait to talk whenever I was ready. Right now, I had let her slide too many times, and I was still allowing her to live under my roof.

"Breeze, let me holla at you."

"Nah, Big Brother, get up with me in the morning," I said as I walked up the stairs. I peeped my head in the twins' room and noticed they were sound asleep. I placed kisses on their little cheeks, then went to my room to shower. My damn feet hurt from standing in those heels all night, but I'd had a damn good time.

"Bruh, why the fuck you sitting on my bed?" Cush was sitting at the foot of my bed when I came out of the bathroom, looking like a madman. Good thing I had a towel wrapped around me.

"Why you just walk off like that when I said I wanted to holla at you?"

"Because I'm not in the mood to talk to Diamond right now."

"Yeah, I get you, sis, and I get you the tough person that hates to be disrespected. But, you a female at the end of the day, and this chip you carry on your shoulder is starting to make one of the most beautiful women in the world, ugly as fuck. I didn't come up here to talk about Diamond, though, because I tried, and you were acting hard. I came up here because I agree with you stepping down now."

"So now you agree?"

"Actually, I been agreed, I just didn't agree with you letting Lou step up. But I saw the way he looked at you, and once I told him you were going to the warehouse with Joc, I saw the way he rushed out the house to protect you. He a nigga, and he fucked up. I don't stand for everything he's done—hell, I know you don't stand for everything I do—but you need to finally have that talk with him."

I listened to everything my brother was saying, and what he didn't know was, I had already planned on hollering at Louis, I just didn't know when would be the right time to talk because we were already so busy.

"But you do need to holla at Diamond. You might understand her anger and aggression more."

"I knew it was a catch," I laughed.

"Nah, but for real, I love you, sis, and I hate to see how mean and ruthless you can be at times."

"I will talk to her soon, let me just holla at Louis first." Once my brother hugged me and left the room, I grabbed something comfy to slip on and got in the bed. The sun was coming up, and I had tossed and turned all night with the things my brother had said on my mind.

I got out the bed with my kids and love on my mind. I shot my shot and went to Louis' room.

When I walked in, he was laying on his stomach, asleep. I admired all the tattoos that graced his back as I got in the bed and snuggled up under him. Louis smelled so good, and his body was so soft, I couldn't help but run my fingers across his back. The moment he rolled over and made eye contact with me, there were no words spoken between us. He grabbed me, placed me on top of him, and hugged me tight as if he didn't want to let go.

I had been fighting myself and my heart for so long, but here with him was where I was supposed to be all along. It was crazy how much hell we had gone through, and all the women he had run through, but my heart was right here with him. As crazy as it might sound to y'all, I knew his heart was with me. I heard the way his heartbeat matched mine as I laid on his chest and traced the tattoo of my portrait. It had been a while, and I wanted him, so with ease, I slid my panties to the side and let him slide his thick, hard dick into my already wet pussy.

"Oooouuuu!" was all he said before I began to make love to him as I rode his every wave. I loved this man so much, and it was crazy how just about everything and everyone had tried to keep us apart. The different obstacles we had gone through had landed us right here.

"Bre, I'm sorry for ever hurting you." I had forgiven him long ago. Even though he had apologized repeatedly, but had still ended up doing the same shit, I knew he was serious this time. The seriousness in his tone, and the eye contact he gave let me know he was serious.

"I love you so much, Lou."

"I love you, too."

We began to kiss passionately as he turned me over and ate me from the back. His tongue alone had my body jerking, but I wanted more of my man. He laid me back on the bed and placed the tip of his dick at my slit before going in, beating my pussy the fuck up. Louis' dick was like no other, and I'd had my share of men. Whenever he entered me, my pussy fit him like a glove.

"Damn, baby, who this pussy for?"

"You, baby. It's for YOUUUUUUUU!" I screamed as I bust what seemed like my third nut.

"FUUUUUUUUK!" Louis released and just laid in me. I wasn't on any type of birth control, and at that moment, I didn't care. I was in the arms of my man, and being with him was the only thing on my mind.

He got off me and went into the bathroom to clean up. He returned to the room with a towel for me and went into the nightstand to get something. I cleaned myself up, then went into the bathroom to shower again. There was nothing like a hot shower after having good sex.

I thanked him for the washcloth, but I needed to feel the water running down my body. I hadn't slept all night, so I grabbed a towel and wrapped it around my body to get in the bed. Later today, I would talk to Louis about everything, but right now, I needed sleep.

"Bre, before you go to sleep, let me talk to you." Lord, I hoped I hadn't just wasted my time with this man.

"What's up?"

"Look, I know I've fucked up and then apologized about it over and over again, but I love you, and I want to be with you. You complete me, and when I'm not with you, I feel like something is missing. I'm thankful for you because you've given me something no other woman has ever given me. I want to make you the happiest woman on Earth. I promised myself if you ever forgave me, I would marry you, so, Breeze McGuy, will you marry me?"

Louis held a rock in his hand so big, I could have passed out. Instead of verbally answering him, I nodded up and down fast. Happy was an understatement. I was relieved, and I was now getting my man. I had prayed long and hard for this moment. We had both done some fucked-up shit, but now it was Breeze, Louis, Cane, and Cali against the world.

I was so excited, I couldn't even go back to sleep after he placed the ring on my finger. I dropped down to my knees and began sucking the skin off my fiancé's dick. I was on a different high right now, and nobody could bring me down. I had everyone behind me, and I would soon forgive Diamond, but I wanted to focus on pleasing my man more than anything.

TWO DAYS HAD PASSED since Louis had popped the question, but I still hadn't told anyone. I had decided to invite everyone out to dinner tonight, and then I would let them know. Cush and I couldn't stay away from each other. After finally waking up from all the sex we had, I decided to go talk to Diamond. I understood her hurt and frustration, but she had to understand mine, too. Everything was straight with us, and if being with Cush was what made her happy, then I was happy for her.

"Do you think everyone is going to be excited once we tell them?" I asked Cush as he stood in front of me, dressed in an all-black button up, black, tight-fitting slacks, and a pair of loafers with gold tips. He was iced the fuck out tonight, and his beard was freshly trimmed. He had left a few buttons unbuttoned, so the tattoos on his chest stood out. If I weren't already dressed, I would have sat on his face.

"Yeah, they know we dysfunctional. You look beautiful, by the way." I could get used to this Louis.

"Come on, let's head out!"

We jumped in my Mercedes G-Wagen and pulled out of the yard. The vibe between us was good, and we matched just right. When Louis and I were in a good place, everything between us was good, but when things were bad, get the fuck back because a hurricane was coming through, and everyone would be affected. But that was how things had always been, and honestly, I wouldn't trade it.

"I love you," he said as he grabbed my hand and kissed the back of it.

"I love you, too."

Tonight, I was going to also tell Louis and everyone else I was stepping down. Since I was now engaged and was at my happiest, it was time to let this life go. Don't get it confused, I was always strapped and wouldn't mind busting that bitch if needed.

Pulling up to the restaurant, my whole gang was dressed nicely, looking like money, and it made me feel like a proud mother. Tip had accepted the fact that we were his siblings, and now he was like my third son. That was our baby, so we made sure he was straight at all times.

We hugged and greeted everyone before going inside and being seated at the table. I'd had Diamond call and rent out the place so we could have the place to ourselves. I sat at the head of the table as Lou sat to the right of me, and Cush to the left. It was a good feeling to have so many loyal people around you who you could call family.

"Hey, everyone, first and foremost I just want to thank you for being such great people in our lives. I know things have been hard and we've lost a lot of family and friends along the way, but I'm happy you all are strong enough to know this is what comes with the game."

"We love you, sis!" I looked at Cush, and he looked so much like Lorez, it was crazy.

"I wanted everyone to come here today because I have an announcement to make. All of y'all here are family, and I wanted to announce that Louis and I are now engaged," I said, then paused to see everyone's reaction before continuing, but we were overwhelmed by all the congrats and hugs. Receiving so much love from so many people was a damn good feeling.

"You guys are making me cry, and y'all know I try not to cry, but I need y'all to know, I'm a mother and about to become a wife. I have been through hell and back with this man, and it's crazy how he has always found a way to make my life better than the day before. Today will be my last day sitting at the head of any table. I'm stepping down, and Louis will now be your supplier. Nothing moves unless he signs for it. But don't get it twisted, I will forever and always be the Queen of Cocaine."

Louis jumped up and kissed me. I knew he was shocked and happy, and the smile my brothers wore let me know I had made the right choice. I hadn't skipped over Tip, either. I'd had a talk with him before the meeting, and he felt he wasn't ready to run an empire on his own. But he would be working directly under Louis.

I switched seats with Louis and let him sit at the head. He smiled the whole time, and I knew things were about to change for him.

"This is now all yours, baby. This is now your empire. Run it with an iron fist!" I spoke those words in his ear as he leaned over and kissed me so hard, I instantly got a funny feeling. The kiss he gave me felt like our last kiss.

I grabbed my purse and began to search through it to see if I had brought my gun. Usually, when I got that feeling, something happened.

Dinner was over, and I walked out of the restaurant with my man, hand in hand, enjoying our friends and laughing up a storm. Things for me couldn't be any better than they were; I was grateful for Louis and everyone around me. I appreciated Cush even more for putting me in my place about the way I had been moving.

"You good?" Louis asked. As I was getting ready to respond, gunshots came out of nowhere. I immediately grabbed my gun out of my purse and began shooting back. I looked the shooter dead in his eyes, and at that moment, I knew my past situations had come back to haunt me.

"Fuck!" I screamed as Louis laid on the ground full of bullets, blood oozing from his body.

"Every time I try and get out, somebody forcefully puts me right back in. Call the paramedics," I said as I walked off.

"Breeze, where the fuck you going?" Both Cush and Tip ran behind me and left Moo and Diamond to look after Lou.

"I'm back in. The whole damn city about to bleed behind this one." I jumped in my car and raced off into traffic.

I really wanted to get out, and I wanted to be happy, but every time I was at my best, somebody just got to come and fuck it up. Niggas had violated and touched my nigga. This whole world was not for him.

I moved in and out of traffic, not thinking about anything but catching up to those coward-ass niggas. Just as I was getting ready to turn, a big truck came out of nowhere and caused me to flip multiple times.

The wheels started rolling in my head. Maybe I should have stayed with my man. I heard Cush's voice but saw Louis' face, and knew I was crossing over. It was crazy how my kids were about to be in the world with no parents. I didn't have to go after those men. I had seen who it was and could have easily sent my bothers. But it was the life I had been so caught up chasing, I just couldn't let go.

I felt my body being lifted out of the car, but there was no more me. I was numb, everything around me was so dark, and every voice I heard was now distant. I didn't see my mother's face this time, and I wondered if I had finally entered my hell.

To be continued...

RR

CPSIA information can be obtained
at www.ICGtesting.com
Printed in the USA
LVHW112102180719
624590LV00001B/108/P

9 781092 946094